HARMON'S WAR

Fleming's town marshal, Rowe Harmon, faces a dilemma: the area's largest rancher, Burke Arnold, plans to drive his cattle through the main street, but a self-appointed preacher is stirring up the womenfolk to prevent it. Then, Arnold discovers someone has been rustling a few of his weaner calves, but he decides to go ahead with the drive — until his daughter goes missing. The marshal and Arnold join forces to track the kidnappers — and that's when the lead begins to fly . . .

Books by Troy Howard
in the Linford Western Library:

THE WIND WAGON
BOOT HILL

TROY HOWARD

HARMON'S WAR

Complete and Unabridged

LINFORD
Leicester

First published in Great Britain in 1999 by
Robert Hale Limited
London

First Linford Edition
published 2000
by arrangement with
Robert Hale Limited
London

British Library CIP Data

Howard, Troy, *1916 –*
Harmon's War.—Large print ed.—
Linford western library
1. Western stories
2. Large type books
I. Title
813.5'4 [F]

ISBN 0–7089–5904–0

Published by
F. A. Thorpe (Publishing)
Anstey, Leicestershire

Set by Words & Graphics Ltd.
Anstey, Leicestershire
Printed and bound in Great Britain by
T. J. International Ltd., Padstow, Cornwall

This book is printed on acid-free paper

1

Making Tracks

Experience makes the difference. After a man acquires enough of it he avoids mistakes unless carelessness intervenes. In Bryan Cullom's case, perfecting a system for branding someone else's cattle required an ideal set of circumstances.

In open range country where the reward is punishment by hanging, cattle theft is not a common or acceptable practice.

If a cowman turns grey practising the rustling occupation it's a lead pipe cinch he is experienced.

For Bryan Cullom who had perfected the procedure, the warm late midday set of circumstances was ideal. For one thing the mammy cow and her calf were enjoying the shade of a grassy swale.

Sunlight hovered a few hours before the sidehills on both sides planted layers of shadowy shade at the bottom of the swale and other critters had grazed along leaving the cow and her overgrown baby well enough isolated for a rustler's purpose.

No cow thief worth his salt rustled branded cattle. Because it was customary for cattle outfits to roundup, overhaul and brand twice a year, in spring and fall the length of time a mammy cow required to go dry, for her calf to be on its own, was commonly quite a few months.

What wasn't common was for a mammy cow to stay with her calf when she no longer had milk, but wasn't exactly uncommon. Maybe the old girl was tenderfooted. What mattered was that conditions were ideal.

For Bryan Cullom the rest of it was as natural as breathing, one piercing look in all directions as he freed his rope and eased forward without haste, dropped his gaze to the 5 – 600 pound slick calf who looked up once with grass stalks protruding from both sides of its mouth, interested but not afraid.

The mammy cow stood like she had taken root and the action was on.

The cow lowed, alternately eyeing her big baby and the man shaking out his loop while his saddle animal balanced forward for its nudge.

The horse took its cue. As it moved in the direction of the calf, Bryan Cullom's rope got slack. The distance closed. A sixty-foot lass rope hung draped. The only movement was the horse. At ten he had perfected what a younger horse would have spoiled; a technique that was close to perfection. He watched the big calf ahead. At fifty feet the cow sashayed and her calf shifted its weight so it was balanced to whirl. At forty feet its mother eased up to break. At the same time the horse felt the rope start upwards which was its signal. It dug in to cover the final distance in a jump. The rope swung twice and paid out as the mammy cow broke to run. Her calf dug in — too late.

The rope came overhand, lost momentum and the calf bawled as dallies took up the slack.

Bryan Cullom left the saddle, lit down hard, reached the calf on the left side, reached far over with both hands and simultaneously bent both knees and hoisted. The calf went off the ground, came down hard and with half the wind knocked out of it could only make a wheeze instead of a bawl. By the time its mother stopped off a ways, Bryan Cullom had the pigging string winding tight. It was too late but the calf fought.

Bryan stood up to briefly watch before walking to the base of a time-battered tree to gather deadfall twigs.

Dead wood made a hot fire without noticeable smoke.

He used his clasp knife to cut a pair of green twigs, removed the running iron from a shirt pocket, threaded the wet limb-wood through so that his grip on the exposed ends closed tightly. It was a satisfactory grip. He dropped the cinch ring into the fire.

It didn't have to be red hot. When he spat on the ring and it sizzled, he rethreaded the green limbs, tested the grip and returned to the calf. It didn't bawl, but when he knelt it fought.

When the stench of burning hair and flesh made a fingerling of smoke arise, the calf finally bawled and fought as hard as it could.

Bryan used his hat to dispel smoke, studied his work and when the calf paused in its struggles he yanked loose the pigging string. The calf sprang up, put its tail over its back and raced to find its mother.

Bryan stamped out the little fire, pocketed the pigging string and watched the cow lead her calf westerly in a dead run.

The only indication of what had happened was a faint lingering scent of burnt hide.

On the way back to his horse, Bryan rolled and lighted a smoke, flicked off sweat and reset his hat. He was breathing hard, the sun had barely moved, some noisy birds in a tree resumed their squabbling over who had the right to make a nest mid-way aloft.

The bay horse stood stone still at the end of the catch rope. He had performed his obligation and was waiting for what came next. The ride north-west where a flake of perfect cured timothy hay and half a coffee tin of rolled barley waited.

His rider coiled the rope as he moved toward the horse. The dallies had come loose. The man coiled as he walked. He would drape the rope, swing astride and go back the way they had come.

Only this time something broke the pattern. When the man was making his last coil he stopped dead still.

On the topout of the westerly hillside a horseman sat like a carving. Bryan could make out the horse; it was a breedy chestnut sorrel with a flaxen mane and tail. It was a leggy animal whose interest in Bryan and the shady depths of his arroyo was fixed to the exclusion of everything else.

The rider sat with loose reins, a sign he had been up there for a fair length of time.

Bryan secured his rope, leaned on his saddle exchanging long stares with the distant rider of the elegant horse. When he was satisfied the stranger had no intention of descending the slope Bryan evened up his reins, said, 'Son of a bitch', swung up over leather and headed up the northerly pass out of his marking ground.

Once he looked back. The chestnut horse and its rider were nowhere in sight.

If they had gone westerly and overtook the cow and calf the rider would notice something Bryan thought he had taken precautions no one would notice for months. The calf had a fresh Sword C on its right ribcage. Its mammy cow was also branded on the right side — B A.

During branding and marking time neither ranchers or their hired riders misbranded livestock.

There were excuses, none of which were satisfactory, and a cowman like old Burke Arnold wouldn't be fooled.

When Bryan got back to the cabin with its peeled-pole corrals and sturdy log barn in its five-acre clearing surrounded by a rugged landscape of forests, grassy meadows, cold water creeks fed by high-country snowmelt, isolation and solitude, he had decided not to mention what had happened miles southward in an arroyo which was part of Burke Arnold's hugely extensive landholdings, where critters wore the B A mark.

It was just as well. Of his two partners, Jack Ballow and Christopher — Chris — Humes, Jack had come out second best in an encounter with a sow bear with twin cubs.

Chris met Bryan in the barn. Both he and Jack were older men, quite a bit older. Neither of them ordinarily showed agitation but with evening close Chris showed it. He helped Bryan care for his horse while explaining that Jack's condition was bad.

During the day Jack lapsed into periods of semi-consciousness. It was Chris's opinion that Jack needed a doctor.

Bryan entered the cabin ahead of Chris, and stopped in his tracks. Of the three bunks, a stranger could have known which belonged to the injured man. Aside from the amount of bloody cloth and the basin with pinkish water the man who had been clumsily bandaged greeted Bryan with a croaking sound of indistinguishable words.

Chris went to stoke the fire, something he did from lifelong habit and repeated from what he had pieced together as he worked.

'He didn't see the old girl until she bellered and charged. He got off one shot. She knocked the rifle out of his hands an' went after him like a cougar.

'He cut her twice with his fleshing knife. She had him on the ground. The noise brought another bear, a boar that tied into the sow. When he went after her cubs she give up on Jack an' went after him. Bryan, fetch your blanket roll from the barn.'

Bryan stood beside the injured older man who tried to smile as he said, 'Buckley, Ma's goin' to scalp you alive. That tom rooster was her pet.'

Chris crossed over. 'See what I mean. Out of his head . . . I bandaged as best I could but he's hurt bad. He needs a medical man.'

Chris's high-pitched voice was irritating. Bryan faced him.

'Out at Fleming they got a buck In'ian that doctors horses. From the looks of him, Chris, he'd never make a day's ride to get down there.'

The tone of the older man's voice changed when he said irritably, 'I know that. What I had in mind, one of us stays with Jack while the other one goes down there, finds the bronco and brings him up here.'

Bryan bent low as the injured man went through a fit of coughing. He straightened up slowly. 'That's blood. He's hurt inside.'

Chris's agitation and irritability increased. 'Boy, I know that! While you been gone all day I been doin' what I could. Boy, he's not goin' to last the night. I've seen 'em busted up before. Coughin' blood . . . '

The man among the bloody blankets struggled to sit up as he loudly said, 'It was an assident. I didn't know it was loaded. I swear it on Momma's grave.'

Bryan let go a rattling sigh. 'Get the whiskey, Chris.'

'I pondered that. It could make him worse.'

Instead of arguing, Bryan went to a crudely made cupboard with harness leather hinges, got a three-quarters full bottle, handed it to Chris and said, 'I'll prop him up.'

Chris put the bottle on a homemade table and glared. 'It'll kill him!'

Bryan scowled. 'He can't make the choice. If he could I'd bet new money he'd want the whiskey. I'll prop him up.'

'I don't think he can swallow. I tried to get some water down him when he come crawlin' through the door.'

Bryan got a handful of flannel shirt. 'When I hold him up, do it!'

'Boy! Take your hand off me!'

The man on the bloody, rumpled bedding choked back a coughing fit and held out a bloody arm where claws had gone bone deep. Bryan pushed Chris aside to place the bottle in the unsteady hand.

Chris scowled and got between them. He would have knocked the bottle away but Bryan struck with his left fist. Chris didn't make a sound until he hit the floor, then he let go with a groan that rattled the door, and turned loose all over.

Bryan stepped over him, put the bottle into Jack's hand and used one arm as a prop. Jack pulled off the cap

12

with his teeth and drank.

Since Bryan had partnered up with the older men he had seen Jack down a third of a bottle and still walk straight.

Chris rolled up onto all fours and groaned when Jack let the bottle fall among his blankets.

Bryan helped him arise, steered him to one of the other bunks and told him to sit there and be quiet.

They had a coal-oil lantern which they rarely used. Candles were cheaper. Bryan lighted four candles and the lantern. Darkness settled outside and stayed out there.

Bryan, who hadn't eaten since the evening before and who had been hungry before he got back, tipped a tin cup half full of coffee, handed it to Chris and emptied what remained in the pot into another cup for himself.

He sat on a three-legged stool at the table, lighted a smoke and ignored it when Chris made an aggrieved statement. 'You didn't have to hit me.'

Bryan pitched the stub of his

brown-paper smoke into the fireplace, lowered his head to his arms atop the table and said, 'Which one of us gets his watch an' chain?'

Chris's response was curt. 'For Chris'sake, he ain't dead yet. You can have 'em. I never learnt to tell time. He spilt that whiskey. Now we're out.'

While Bryan slept, Chris removed everything from Jack's pockets. That's how he knew Jack was dead.

He left Bryan asleep at the table, took everything of Jack's including his guns, money, horse and saddle and rode through what remained of the night and camped beside a hilltop creek where he could see in all directions.

About an hour before dawn he was in the saddle, leading Jack's horse with a full pack in the direction of that town called Fleming.

He had neglected to raid the food box, an oversight he would regret before he saw the church steeple amid rooftops which amounted to the only break in an otherwise seemingly endless

14

virgin territory as far as a man could see.

Jack's horse, unaccustomed to the role of a pack animal, hung back on the lead shank each time the clumsy, hurriedly made load shifted. The last time it did this Chris was passing through downhill country.

He had to stop, readjust the pack, call the horse names and resume the trail until he entered Fleming and had occasion to once again turn the air blue. It wasn't the horse this time. He had angled westerly to reach the roadway when a stage and six came out of nowhere in a loose lope and spewed dust enough to make a man's eyes water.

The driver raised his silver ferruled whip in a high wave which Chris did not return.

The livery barn was beyond the tanyard at the lower end of town. The proprietor was a bowlegged man about Chris's age, which was in the late fifties or maybe the middle sixties. He was a short individual with a strawberry nose and ears twice as large as they should have been.

His name was Jackson Barton. Jackson wasn't really his first name. He had served a Secesh general named Thomas Jonathon Jackson, the liveryman's lifelong hero.

Chris put up the horses, told the liveryman he figured to stay a few days in Fleming and seemed to briefly falter when the liveryman welcomed him to Fleming by introducing himself.

'It's a right nice place, friend. Since we'll likely do business my name is Jackson Barton. Folks call me Jack.'

Chris shook the extended hand, nodded and went in search of an eatery of which Fleming had two, both run by widow-women.

The liveryman was right, a man could do worse than to settle for a spell in a place like Fleming.

It wasn't large, more likely a village than a town, but aside from a church with a high steeple painted stark white, there were also several businesses including the Blue Duck Saloon and Hersheimer's general store and emporium with an inventory in some ways larger than that of general stores in regular towns.

Also, Fleming was the main way station of the Fleming Stage and Cartage Company which hauled freight and operated two daily stage runs, one northerly and one southerly.

Fleming's town marshal had a splendidly drooping thick moustache. He had once seen a lithograph of Buffalo Bill Cody who wore such facial adornment and it had taken him a full year to grow a duplicate, but he had accomplished it.

His name was Rowe Harmon. He was well over six feet tall, weighed in at no less than 200 pounds and what difficulties he couldn't handle with his fists he could top off with his belt-gun, a fine piece with ivory grips and the initials R H engraved on the butt plate.

He was a likeable individual, helpful

around town, not easily roiled but if something upset him folks discreetly selected places out of his path.

Marshal Harmon had been courting a widow-woman named Alice Gordon since about the time she opened her café.

Like other small settlements, folks managed to know things and one of them was Alice Gordon's approval of Rowe Harmon, who had lost his wife years back in a bar-room fire back in bloody Kansas.

By the time Chris Humes had been in Fleming three days he knew almost as much of the local story-telling as was worth knowing.

He didn't learn much from burly Alice who had a complexion like peaches and cream and very dark eyes that stirred things in menfolk that were better left dormant.

Chris ignored the other eatery, run by a wizened gnome of a female with a tongue that could lash the hide off a green-broke mule.

Against his better judgement Chris lingered beyond his three days, something that tickled the liveryman. Like a few others who had nothing better to do than watch Alice's single bachelor trade, Jackson Barton swapped snippets of gossip about the stranger's probable infestation of worms that drove him to eat a meal punctually three times a day at Alice Gordon's café.

By the time a full week had passed and there was a taste of autumn in the air, Jackson Barton's cronies were betting good money the marshal and the stranger were on the way to locking horns, but beyond betting it would happen no one offered to make a wager about the outcome. Rowe Harmon was four inches and a full hand taller than Chris and easily a muscled-up thirty pounds heftier.

The only thing that could replace this interesting item was when word arrived that old Burke Arnold's annual autumn cattle drive had come south as far as a big clearing known as Firewood Camp.

Arnold's four full-time rangemen, plus the old man himself and sometimes Miss Elise, the old man's daughter, penned cattle beyond the far south country before beginning the final fifty-mile trek to the railroad siding corrals down at Clausberg.

The drive was an annual affair, had been for some eighteen or twenty years.

Burke's riders spent money in town. It placated the folks who complained that cattle, fresh off green feed, shouldn't be allowed to use Fleming's wide main thoroughfare.

2

Questions and Answers

The B A drive was coming; there was no turning it back so the two factions whose concern was uppermost began their campaigns. Those folks in opposition to having cattle on green feed using Fleming's main road and the others who treated the Burke Arnold cattle drive as some kind of annual festival, met at the firehouse which was two doors north of Edgar Bemis's saddle and harness works. Ed Bemis was in his late twenties. He had inherited the leather works from an expired uncle, an unpleasant old gaffer whose command of profanity was awesome in an area where swearing was an art form.

What had shocked the whey out of Fleming's inhabitants was that when young Bemis had arrived to take over his inheritance he made it clear that he was a man of God, a pronouncement which had been met with mixed concern.

The long neglected Fleming firehouse was taken over by the harness-maker, who was responsible for the church and for its steeple being painted white, the symbol of purity.

The firehouse meetings, rarely held, were for the purpose of discussing and if possible settling differences.

Prior to the arrival of Ed Bemis, meetings had been presided over by Marshal Rowe Harmon who had gladly relinquished that distinction in favour of the preacher, something that did not sit well with everyone. Fleming was one of those frontier places where newcomers were looked upon with general wariness. The fact that Bemis had settled in three years prior to the latest firehouse meeting did not entirely ameliorate the wary standoffishness.

The marshal sat near the only doorway when the harness-making preacher called things to order.

Rowe expected trouble as did others, but when young Bemis established a precedent by opening the meeting with a prayer, a lot of the starch went out of those present who had arrived prepared to raise hell and prop it up.

The identical arguments of dispute that had been raised before were raised again. Several cowmen put forth harangues favouring Burke Arnold's right by precedent to drive his animals wherever he elected to drive them.

The 'No Scouring Cattle In Our Town' faction objected on the same grounds they'd always used. Health issues and the unpleasant obligation old Burke Arnold forced the decent law-abiding citizens of Fleming to be careful where they stepped when crossing the roadway.

The meeting lasted well past bed-time, Fleming was a community addicted to candlelight. Better lighting was provided by lamps and lanterns but coal oil was expensive.

Nothing was settled. With this issue nothing had ever been settled. The final half-hour was passed with anger and enough profanity to induce the preacher-saddle-and-harness-maker to out shout everyone, beat the tabletop with a gavel and call upon the Almighty to forgive those in attendance whose use of blasphemous profanity required forgiveness.

Two days later, Burke Arnold and his range boss, a leathery-faced life-long stockman named Josh Davidson entered town from the north. The cattle, the wagon and the other riders were striking camp about six miles from Fleming. Burke Arnold gave Jake Hersheimer at the emporium a list of supplies for the trail-wagon which would arrive in town ahead of the drive.

At the Blue Duck Saloon he said he would hold back the drive north of town and string it out through Fleming in the morning.

Burke and the marshal visited at the jailhouse where a scrap of information was mentioned that made the marshal straighten up in his chair. He said, 'Seven head?'

Burke nodded, crossed one leg over the other and looked steadily at Rowe Harmon. 'There may be more but when we made the cut there was seven head.' Burke made a humourless, wry smile. 'Our B A on the cow, right side, and some kind of knife, a dagger or maybe a sword on the calf.'

'Calf on the right side too?'

Arnold nodded. 'A long weaner. Another few weeks an' they'd have separated.'

'Anythin' else?'

Burke uncrossed his legs, settled back on the bench and fished for the makings. As he was building his smoke he said, 'Not sure of the connection, Rowe, but Josh picked up sign an' tracked it to a log house in the foothills . . . with a dead man in it.' Burke lit up, fished in a pocket, placed a crumpled scrap of paper on the marshal's table and said, 'That's directions to the shack. Josh thinks there was three of 'em. He scouted up a small band of short two year olds with that same brand on 'em. Wild as deer. Josh figured there might be more, but it was gettin' along so he headed for home.'

Burke stood up, killed his smoke in a bowl of stubs and reset his hat. 'There was sign of someone ridin' a horse, leadin' one goin' north. There was sign of a third one, the feller my daughter watched put that knife C on one of our B A slicks. The slick we mammied up with a B A cow.'

'Any sign where that third one might be, Burke?'

'All I can tell you is what Josh told me. That third one was ridin' a horse only shod in front. His sign went due north into the trees. Josh came back.'

Rowe also stood up. 'I'd like to see the misbranded ones.'

'Ride out, Rowe. I'm goin' back. I'll have 'em cut out for you.'

At the door, Burke Arnold also said, 'Someone set up in the foothills to start up in the rustlin' business. They're pretty *coyote*; only rustle long yearlings that we wouldn't brand until the fall gather. Rowe . . . ?'

The marshal waited.

'Elise saw one of 'em. From what she told me he wasn't a greenhorn. He used a cinch ring for a brandin' iron. That much she could make out from a distance. There was no handle to his iron so it had to be a runnin' iron. A cinch ring. She watched him make a fire to heat the iron. It wasn't a regular brandin' iron, there wasn't a long handle. Ride out, Rowe, we'll be waitin'. It'll be dark directly, don't put it off too long.'

Rowe had no intention of delaying his departure from town. As he rode he pondered. To his knowledge no other cowman had mentioned misbranded critters. That pretty well limited the activities of these particular individuals. But he'd ask around. The difficulty here would be the same as it was with Burke Arnold; misbranded animals would not

27

show up for another month or more when roundups were undertaken. This particular problem wouldn't have shown up either if it hadn't been Burke's custom to make a drive before the others got around to it.

He heard cattle bawling long before he saw dust mingling with late afternoon's lowering sun off in the west.

The bawling was caused by gummer cows among the better quality critters that made up the drive. Their agitation resulted from horsemen singling out a few head and trying to hold them away from the other cattle.

Burke was waiting. His range boss was with him, reins looped while he rolled and lit a brown-paper cigarette.

Josh was too occupied to wave but Burke wasn't. He met the marshal where the agitation and bawling was worst. They had to yell to one another.

Burke left his range boss with another rider, rode a slow circle around several big, marketable critters that looked to be slightly shy of being two year olds. They were in prime flesh. Their racket added to the noise the cull cows were making. They moved constantly, were prevented from breaking clear to rejoin the other cattle. Among the B A riders keeping them from breaking away was Burke Arnold's daughter who was as experienced as the men. She ignored her father and the marshal.

Rowe reined into position for his purpose. He saw three of the animals Burke had mentioned to him back in town.

The brands were readable without much effort. He finished sashaying back and forth, reined clear and went to join Burke, who shook his head and led off to get further from the turmoil. He wig-wagged with his hat and his daughter left a gap on the east side of the surround. The big animals with the strange brand took full advantage of the opening to head for the main gather.

Burke dismounted out a ways, waited until his companion did the same then said, 'Satisfied, Rowe?'

'Plumb satisfied, Burke, but before I go man-hunting I got to know if any other outfits have got misbranded animals, an' somethin' else: are they misbranded, stolen cattle or maybe some as been bought an' haven't been maybe road branded, or someone's got a bill of sale for 'em.'

Burke used his hat to get rid of a ground wasp that was trying to bore through his boot top.

'I already did that, Rowe. Sent Josh and the boys all over hell askin' questions.' He paused to stamp the wasp, made sure it was dead and to reset his hat. 'No such thing as cattle with that knife C mark. Not within fifty miles in all directions. The reason I did that was because you'd want to know. Me, I'm satisfied those three fellers up yonder with their little bunch of my short two year olds wearin' that sword C, or whatever they'd call it, is fixin' to start up in the rustling business.'

Rowe remounted and evened up his

reins before speaking again. 'What can they do with no more'n maybe a dozen or so stolen big calves? Feed 'em up for a year an' trail them out to sell?'

'You missed somethin', Rowe. They're all heifers. Just for the hell of it let's say you'n me wanted to set up in the cattle business. If we was savvy we'd find land no one'd be likely to visit . . . it'd take time; three, four years an' we'd have a start. Another few years of rustlin' unbranded heifers an' we'd be on our way.' Burke considered the dawning look of incredulity on his friend's face and shook his head. 'If it's not that, what is it? You'n I would look for a place like where Josh found that dead man. Hell, Rowe. If Elise hadn't seen that feller with a runnin' iron an' if Josh wasn't born with a curiosity bump as big as a watermelon . . . All right, Rowe, go on back to town, have a couple at the Blue Duck, eat up hearty at Alice Gordon's place an' come up with an alternative that fits. Meanwhile I'll finish the drive down to Clausberg. I can't ship out those runnin'-iron critters. I got no bill of sale for 'em so I got to bring 'em back, or maybe peddle them to a butcher who don't ask questions. I'll see you when I get back. Do me a favour. Don't sit on your butt while I'm gone.'

By the time the marshal got back to town it was close enough to dark for lights to be showing.

He put up his horse at Jackson Barton's livery barn, went to the jailhouse to sit in shadows until hunger drove him to Alice's eatery, which wasn't exactly crowded, but where he had to wait until the leatherman-preacher nodded on his way out before he could find a place at the counter; the bench was still warm.

He didn't visit around which was customary where men gathered to eat and relax.

He only showed a spark of interest when Jack Barton came in smelling like someone who just finished dunging out horse stalls, sat down next to the marshal and, after a few pleasantries to which he got no response, said, 'Marshal, I got a question. You know that feller that hangs around Miss Alice's café? Stranger. He told me he figured to lie over for three days or so; you know who I mean?'

Rowe shook his head, drained his cup of black java and leaned to arise.

Jack said, 'I forget names, but he come ridin' in leadin' a pack animal some weeks back.'

Rowe relaxed on the counter's bench. 'What about him? His name's Chris Humes.'

The liveryman paused long enough to give Alice his order before speaking again. 'For one thing he wasn't leadin' no pack animal. It had a pack but it was a couple of blankets, one with blood on it. An' he had two carbines one with claw marks on it, shy one load.'

Rowe smiled when Alice refilled his cup and she smiled back. Jack ignored these pleasantries. 'He had someone's six-gun with initials cut into the grips, J

B.' Barton leaned close and lowered his voice. 'There's a stinkin' sock half full of greenbacks.'

Rowe fished out the makings, offered them to Barton who shook his head. He wasn't a smoker he was a chewer. He lowered his voice another notch. 'Eighty-six dollars in the sock. Some of it's crumpled and stiff . . . with blood.'

Barton leaned back, pulled down a deep breath and fixed the lawman with a narrow-eyed look. 'You want to come down with me? I'll show you.'

Rowe trickled smoke. 'Jack, how come you to go through that feller's belongings?'

The air left Barton's cheeks. 'That don't have anythin' to do with what I'm tellin' you. There's blood, dried an' stiff.'

Rowe finished his coffee, winked at Alice who winked back, jerked his head and led off southward to the livery barn where the liveryman took him inside the harness-room.

Rowe stopped dead still. There were

scattered blankets, a pair of Winchesters leaning against the wall and a six-gun with the blueing worn off on the liveryman's rickety little table. He examined the six-gun first, took the sock being held out to him, dug out the contents, counted it, smoothed out the notes that were stiff with something that could have been old dried blood and could just as easily be stiff from some other cause, killed his smoke in a tin cup half full of water, sat down at the desk and looked steadily at the liveryman, who fidgeted under the stare and said, 'He's murdered someone and robbed him. Or maybe he robbed him first. There's enough blood to bleed out a boar pig. What do you think?'

Rowe stood up, he was tired. 'Put that stuff back exactly as you got it.' Barton was agreeable. 'An' don't say a word. Suppose Humes comes for his animals and leaves town? He'll know you been pryin'.'

Rowe reached the door before he also

said, 'Sleep tight, Jack,' and left the barn in the direction of the rooming-house where he'd lived since arriving in Fleming.

Sleep didn't come easily: first some damned cattle rustling. Maybe. It was possible there was a valid reason for those B A calves being misbranded. He'd have to satisfy himself about that. Then there was this matter of bloody blankets, a horse that wasn't broke to packing and a sock almost full of money.

He knew Chris Humes. By now just about everyone in Fleming knew him, including the old man who had a barber shop and who knew everyone, and everything.

He awakened the following morning with some bits and pieces already formed in his head.

He rigged out and rode north to see Burke Arnold's range boss and maybe Elise Arnold too.

The range boss was out tracking some bunch-quitters who'd left the gather some time in the night. Burke was nursing a sore knee so he gave Rowe directions, but did not ride with him.

Bunch quitters usually headed for home pastures. Rowe, and the range boss were lucky. These bunch-quitters were old gummer cows that hadn't travelled fast or far. One reason was a rawboned old brindle cow with tender feet. The others set their pace to her gimpy gait.

Josh had already found the old girls and was driving them back. Where he met the marshal was near a piddling little creek where the cows had deferred to the brindle cow who had gone to stand in the mud.

Josh Davidson was as surprised to meet the lawman as Rowe was to meet him.

Rowe dismounted as did the range boss. Rowe wasted no time, he wanted to know as much as Josh could tell him about the log shack with the dead man in it.

Josh Davidson was a taciturn individual. He related what he had seen and ended up with a question.

'There's another one: all I can say about him is that his horse is only shod in front. It was gettin' along or I'd have tracked him further. I turned back for home when his sign got hard to read for pine an' fir needles an' I was goin' to miss supper if I didn't give up an' head back.'

Rowe plucked a grass stalk and was plucking it to chew when he said, 'Which way was he headin' when you left him?'

'North, an' maybe a tad easterly. If he kept to that trail he'd pass Fleming about a mile or such a matter northerly. It'd be timber country for one hell of a distance; until he come out on B A meadowland, but I'd guess he'd change direction. There's no horse feed, Marshal. Not until he got to our range.'

Rowe was ready to mount up when he asked his last question. 'How do I find the log house?'

'From town?' Josh knelt, smoothed ground with a twig and went to work. 'Go south of town . . . you know where Pilgrim Rock is?'

Rowe nodded. 'In'ians had a camp there years back. The back of the rock's burnt black from cookin' fires.'

Josh tossed the twig away and stood up. 'There's what used to be a trail south of there maybe a quarter of a mile. Take that old trail, keep goin' until you come to a piddlin' creek. Follow it south. There's a clearin'; the log house sets at the southerly end. Marshal, if that dead man's still in the house you'll want to stay outside, the weather's been warm lately.'

As Rowe mounted Josh wagged his head. 'If the one that's missin' is still up in there you keep a sharp watch.'

After the marshal left, taking a thoughtful long route back to town, the range boss skived off a cud, pouched it in one cheek and spat. It was too late now. He should've thought of it before. Why would the marshal want to find that cabin?

Rowe couldn't have provided the range boss with a sensible answer. If he'd mentioned wakening out of a dream the night before Josh would have regarded him from an expressionless face.

Alice had kept the stew hot. When Rowe walked in she dished him up a meal and leaned back against the pie table regarding him. 'Something bothering you?' she asked.

He finished chewing and swallowed before answering and was almost distracted by the way she was standing with both arms crossed.

'Burke Arnold's got some misbranded heifers,' he said, and Alice nodded.

'Elise was in a while back. She mentioned that.'

As she moved to clear away his plate he said, 'Would you like to go buggy ridin' this evening?'

She was refilling his coffee cup, eyes on what she was doing when she answered. 'I was going to wash my hair tonight.'

Rowe's little smile congealed. 'It looks right nice to me.'

She turned to put the coffee pot on the pie shelf and had her back to him when she said, 'What time? It takes me an hour to clean up the kitchen.' She turned to face him. Whatever might have happened didn't. A freshly shaved and sheared Chris Humes came in. His smile went over the marshal's head. As he approached the counter he said, 'The moon's almost full tonight . . . I can get old Barton's top buggy . . . ?'

Alice got a little colour in her face as she said, 'Tonight's when I wash my hair.'

She moved her gaze to the seated marshal as though she wanted to say something but Chris spoke first.

'Maybe tomorrow night.' He smiled. 'The moon'll still be up there.'

She picked up the soiled plates and disappeared beyond a curtain with improbably large cabbage roses on it.

41

Both men left the café. They neither spoke nor nodded. Chris struck out for the Blue Duck saloon. Marshal Harmon crossed over and walked south to reserve the liveryman's fringed-top light buggy.

3

In Search of a Dead Man

For the preceding ten or twelve years Burke Arnold had made the first autumn cattle drive southward through Fleming and beyond. A number of towns-folk looked forward to this event, about an equal number opposed what was well on the way of becoming a tradition and someday they would force a change but not for some years to come.

Rowe and others whose primary concern was the town's welfare had made a point of being available until the last critter and rider had passed well southward.

It bothered him; he couldn't be in two places at once, but he wanted very much to hunt up that log house Josh Davidson had mentioned. As

Alice had said last night during their buggy ride he did not absolutely have to be in town when the drive passed through.

She was right there was a possibility he wouldn't be needed in town. B A's riders were rarely troublesome. Later when Burke Arnold tied up out front, his drive about a mile northward, the marshal accepted the cigar Arnold offered and made his decision. He would go up yonder.

For some reason he couldn't have satisfactorily explained to himself he left town by the back alley on the west side behind the livery barn where Jackson Barton watched him. Old Barton wasn't given to premonitions which was just as well. It was a beautiful autumn day without a cloud in the sky and excepting a low, fitful, occasional light wind that stirred roadway dust, by the time he rode past Indian Rock he was raising a light sweat.

Finding the turn-off Josh Davidson

had mentioned was not difficult because he was watching for it.

At eight years of age his grulla gelding was in his prime, otherwise he might have resented having to leave flat country.

If successive generations of Indians hadn't made the trail moderately readable Rowe wouldn't have been able to reach the first plateau before the sun was directly overhead.

He stopped at a cold-water creek, loosened the cinch, hobbled the horse and removed its bridle so it could crop grass, which was rank and green for a fair distance on both sides of the watercourse and as dry as straw everywhere else.

It was at the creek he caught the first faint scent of burning wood. He sashayed out a ways on foot, saw no smoke and went back to rig out and ride southward.

There were scattered meadows, some with old, dried cattle sign. Without any idea where the log house was located he meandered easterly and westerly. In the places where old forest giants blocked out both the sun and the terrain, he sought fringes and once he arrived at a place where someone had downed trees and assumed, since it was too far from town in country too rugged for firewood hunters to drive the stripped-down wagons woodcutters used, he thought he was getting close to either the clearing of the log house the range boss had mentioned, or he'd arrived where a lightning strike had consummated Mother Nature's thinning process.

Where huge old overripe pines and firs hindered visibility, he had trouble locating the sun's position and since he did not own a watch he could only guess how much of this day he had wasted so far.

He came around a long-spending slope of forest so densely wooded he might have lost all idea of direction except for an instinct not everyone possessed; he had never been able to explain how he instinctively knew directions.

He finished half circling the sidehill, saw sunlight ahead and reined toward it. Where the trees were thin he saw the meadow, and southward, secluded by shadows as though deliberately positioned where it would not be readily visible, a log house with a log barn and an accompanying large corral made of draw-knifed fir poles.

He drew rein within the final assortment of fir giants, looped his reins and sat like a carving admiring what he saw.

The structures were not only sturdily made but where corners were required someone had mitred the joints with admirable perfection.

Cattle thieves or not, whoever was responsible for those structures and their corral was either an experienced woodworker or a perfectionist. Maybe a little of both.

The first time the horse heard it and pointed his ears. The second time Rowe heard it. Somewhere behind the barn which cut off the view someone was hacking wood, not with the powerful overhang blows of a wood splitter, more like someone making kindling.

He left the grulla tied, unshipped his saddle gun and went carefully and soundlessly ahead, keeping the barn between himself and whoever was on the far side of it.

He had to cross open country when he was opposite the log house which was ticklish business. He could have turned back. That decision was made for him when a horse sounded somewhere north-west of the barn and was answered by the grulla.

The noise behind the barn stopped. Rowe eased behind a pair of splits — two trees growing from the same root system.

Time passed. He saw nor heard nothing more. It occurred to him that whoever was over there had heard his horse and most probably would be intent on finding it.

In order to do that the phantom would have to cross the same open terrain Rowe had avoided.

He made himself comfortable and waited. For both of them it was the same; someone had to move, either Rowe would go back or the other person would move into the open territory.

There was one flaw to this idea: Rowe was in unfamiliar territory, the other man wasn't.

It was the whistle that made Rowe freeze. It had come from behind him. He had been watching in the wrong direction, his adversary had gone southward using trees down in that direction to shelter movement. When he was far enough in that direction he had crossed over and had come stealthily up behind Rowe who was protected by the splits in front.

The invisible man's voice had no intonation of fear when he said, 'Stand up, mister. Lean the carbine aside. Don't face around. Just stand up.'

Rowe left the saddle gun and arose. The next command came in the same almost too-calm a voice.

'Who are you an' what're you doin' up here?'

Rowe answered in the same tone of voice. 'I'm the marshal from down at Fleming, south-east of here a fair distance.'

'I know where Fleming is. What're you doin' up here?'

That wasn't as easy to answer. 'Nosing around,' Rowe replied and gave his adversary no chance to retort. 'I'm lookin' for someone who rides a horse that's only shod in front.'

'Why? What's he wanted for?'

'Far as I know he's not wanted.'

'Marshal, I know who you are. I've seen you down yonder. Once more, what're you nosin' around up here for?'

Rowe replied curtly. 'I'm lookin' for a dead man.'

That remark held the invisible man temporarily speechless. 'Are you now? What made you think there'd be a dead man up here?'

Rowe said, 'Mind if I face around?'

'I mind; stay the way you are. Who told you there was a dead man up here an' how'd you find the house?'

Rowe's retort was caustic. 'Mister, I'm gettin' tired of this. You got the drop. All I want is answers.'

The man holding a pointed Winchester gave another delayed response. 'All right, shed the pistol an' turn around.'

Rowe emptied his hip holster as he faced around. He wasn't certain but the man opposite him looked vaguely familiar. He said, 'My name's Rowe Harmon.'

The man facing him made a curt nod. 'I know. What're you up in here for?'

'I already told you. What's your name?'

This time the barest hint of a humourless smile showed when the man answered. 'Joe Smith.'

Rowe spat, looked for something to sit on and went to a stump. From there he considered the lean, youngish-looking stranger as he said, 'You need a shave, Joe. How long you been skulkin' around up in here?'

'I ask the questions, Marshal. Someone told you how to find this place? There was a rangeman pokin' around some time back. Was it him?'

Rowe fished out the makings and went to work without looking up. 'Joe, how come you only shoe your horse in front?'

Smith inhaled deeply as cigarette smoke was carried in his direction and Rowe grinned as he tossed over his sack with the papers. 'A man kind of misses 'em, don't he? Joe, put up the carbine. I got no gun. Let's talk.'

The carbine was leaned aside as Joe Smith went to work making a smoke using both hands. When he deeply inhaled and exhaled his gaze toward Rowe was different. The hostility showed less.

He said, 'You carry a belly-gun, Marshal?'

'Nope. Nor a boot knife. Sit down, Joe.'

Smith remained standing and the tie-down over his six-gun was still in place, but after a few moments he yanked it loose and sat on the ground. 'There was that rangeman who tracked me. I watched until he turned back. He's the one you talked to, yes?'

Rowe nodded. 'Him an' others. Where's the dead man, Joe?'

'Buried behind the barn, outside the corral westerly a ways.'

'Who was he?'

'It don't matter. He was out huntin' an' got caught by a sow bear with cubs.'

'Did he have a name?'

'Jack Ballow. Here, thanks for the smoke.'

'Keep it. I got one in my saddle pocket. Joe, you mind if I ask you a personal question?'

'Yeah, I mind . . . what is it?'

'Your left shirt pocket; it's got the outline of a cinch ring in it. Another question, Joe; did you see that woman sittin' on a horse watchin' you or one of your friends brandin' a big B A calf with some kind of a knife mark an' the letter C?'

Joe Smith's gaze widened. 'A woman? That was a woman up there?'

Rowe dropped his smoke and ground it under his boot. When he looked up he wasn't smiling. 'It was a female woman, the daughter of Burke Arnold whose brand was on the heifer's mammy cow.' Rowe leaned to stand up.

Joe Smith palmed his side arm. 'Set back down!'

Rowe sat down. Joe Smith did not holster his hand-gun, he asked a question. 'That's why you're nosin' around up here?'

Rowe avoided an honest answer. He drily said, 'In your boots I'd be a hunnert miles from here. You had a reason for stayin'?'

Joe Smith eased his hat brim slightly to avoid the oblique sunshine. He was silent for a long while before speaking again. 'I ought to shoot you, only that'd stir things up down in Fleming; they'd come huntin' you. I got one grave out back of the corral; I don't like the notion of diggin' another one.'

'What's his name, Joe?'

'It don't matter. When a man's dead nothin' matters . . . I told you his name: Jack Ballow.'

'There was three of you. Ballow's buried, you're sittin' in front of me. Where's the other one?'

Joe had smoked the quirly until it almost burned his fingers. He spat in his palm to douse the quirly and spoke. 'He left. I tracked him a ways, when it got dark I came back.'

Rowe had nothing to lean against so he got down on the ground and used the stump for a back rest. He had only a vague idea of the time, it didn't really matter.

He was unarmed facing a man who was armed and who without much doubt was a cattle rustler.

Joe broke the hush. 'Go back, Marshal, I'm about through here; I'll be ridin' on. I don't know what you come up here for, but I can tell you Jack's dead, Chris's gone an' you'n me will never meet again. After today I'll be as far off as a man can go an' keep right on ridin'. You come here to arrest someone? For what?'

Rowe jutted his jaw. 'You should've thrown that runnin' iron into a canyon. Burke Arnold's got your misbranded heifers. If I know him he'll put a bounty on you sure as we're sittin' here.' Rowe paused a moment. 'Who is Chris?'

Joe Smith seemed startled. His slip of the tongue had been totally inadvertent. 'It don't matter. By now he's so far from here . . . '

Rowe audibly sighed and wagged his head. 'Chris . . . Humes?'

Joe nodded. 'He took Ballow's gun, horse'n money. Least he could've done was divide the money. I had no use for the other things. I already got a horse an' my guns are better.'

Rowe stood up and dusted off. 'Joe,

was it Chris misbranded the B A heifers?'

Joe also stood up. He fished in a shirt pocket, brought forth the cinch ring and handed it to the marshal. 'It belonged to Chris. The whole thing was his idea. Ask that woman. She could most likely identify that feller she watched from up yonder.'

Rowe held the cinch ring on the palm of his hand. It had clearly been used often.

Joe said, 'You knew Chris?' and when Rowe nodded, Joe spoke confidently. 'You'll never catch him. Chris's wanted from Texas to hell an' gone.'

Rowe let the cinch ring slip from his fingers, it rolled twice and came to rest not far from the scuffed toes of Joe's feet. When he instinctively bent to retrieve it, Rowe hit him alongside the head and afterwards stepped over Joe to recover his belt-gun and the Winchester.

When Joe recovered he got up on to all fours and scrabbled in the dirt with both hands. The marshal leaned, pushed a cold gun muzzle in Joe's ear and said, 'Stand up!'

The downed man had to be helped. Anyone back down in Fleming could have told him that when the marshal hit someone they couldn't remember which way was up for several hours.

They went to the cabin. Because the place needed an airing Rowe left the door open.

The captive began to talk. It was almost as though he needed to do this.

Rowe listened. He examined the blood-stiff bunk where a man had died. Otherwise there was little that interested him except his companion, who hadn't been living in the log house. He had a camp in an adjoining meadow.

Rowe wanted to get back to town. His prisoner's horse and outfit were about a half-mile distant in the other meadow. The day had worn along. By Rowe's estimate they wouldn't reach Fleming until nightfall. He helped his prisoner make a gathering which was tied behind the prisoner's cantle. By the time they started back, the woodlands they had to pass through were developing shadows. There wasn't much conversation. Rowe's interest in the man his prisoner blamed for his own trouble went well beyond what the prisoner said.

Rowe's real interest was in the man his prisoner had inadvertently named. There was another bother: during the long ride back he tried to imagine a valid reason for taking Humes into custody. As far as he knew now the man had done nothing except perhaps rob a dead man. Unless he'd also used the cinch ring on Burke Arnold's heifers.

By the time they left the forested uplands, Rowe's interest in Chris Humes had got him involved in another verbal outburst and the more his prisoner talked the less Rowe was inclined to believe him; but he listened, 'Chris's got female mania. He chases after female women like most men go after cold beer on a hot day. He kept me'n Jack awake dang near all night one time tellin' us about the women he'd got hold of.'

When they left the trail and met the stage road, a northbound coach went past. It was being pulled by tired horses in a weary trot. The whip saluted the marshal with his whip. This time Rowe returned the wave.

They went up the west-side alley to enter the livery barn. There was no sign of the liveryman. As they were off-saddling, Rowe thought Barton was probably having supper.

There was no wheeled traffic and only a few people were using the plankwalks. Rowe got his prisoner to the jailhouse where he lighted the overhead lamp, gestured for his prisoner to sit and sank down at his desk, which was actually a table without more than two drawers.

Rowe watched the prisoner roll and light a cigarette and spoke while putting the cinch ring beside his hat on the table.

The ring was still perfectly round although there was evidence it had been heated in many fires.

The prisoner suddenly said, 'It's not Joe Smith: it's Bryan Cullom.'

Rowe put the running iron aside, leaned on the table top and eyed his prisoner. 'Bryan, that cinch ring could get you hanged.'

Bryan Cullom inhaled and exhaled before answering. 'How? That woman was off a hell of a distance.'

'Her father's range boss tracked you. You were ridin' a horse only shod in front.'

'It'd take more'n that, Marshal.'

'Not if her father gets his hands on you. Him an' his tough old range boss most likely hung their share of rustlers. They been in the business since before there was any law in this country.'

The prisoner ground out his smoke under one boot. 'How about you, Marshal? I'll tell you somethin' you most likely already know. The authority of a town marshal don't go no further than the town's limits.' Cullom made a hard little smile. 'I run into this before down in New Messico. You got to be a sheriff, or the army, to hold a person. You're not either.'

Rowe waited until a noisy freight wagon had passed before speaking again. 'You said Humes was a rustler over in Idaho.'

'That's what he told me'n Jack. He had an idea how to get into the ranchin' business without gettin' caught. Jack liked it. Me, I wasn't sure I wanted to wait to get branded heifers old enough to calve. Jack said he was tired of buckin' the law. He liked the idea . . . we went along.'

'How many big heifers did you mark that belonged to someone else?'

'We were just gettin' started. Chris marked four, I marked three.'

'Whose idea was it to use the runnin' iron?'

'Chris's. He used it for a couple of years an' sold off the critters he mis-marked.'

'How did Jack Ballow die?'

'I told you; went huntin' an' got mauled by a sow bear with cubs.'

Rowe leaned back off the table. He was both hungry and tired. As he arose he said, 'Stand up. Through that door.'

Locking up his rustler was no problem. That came when Bryan Cullom complained about being hungry.

Rowe said he'd attend to that, locked Cullom in, returned to his office, doused the lantern, scooped up a key ring, locked the jailhouse from the outside and headed for Alice's café.

It was crowded. Supper-time for single men could be anytime. Several diners greeted the marshal with nods. One in particular, seated at the furthest section of the counter, next to the kitchen, nodded. It was Chris Humes. The marshal nodded back.

4

Another Day

Alice took the lawman's order. Rowe assumed her obvious brusqueness was the result of having so many diners lined up at her counter. She barely more than glanced at her latest customer.

Three diners who had an argument going left Rowe with the impression they had been up at the saloon. Two were rangemen, the third man was the liveryman, Jackson Barton. He was loudly of the opinion that B A cattle should not be allowed to use the town's main thoroughfare on their drive south.

The argument had clearly been in progress before the town's lawman entered the café. After his arrival the dispute became louder and more aggravated.

When Alice brought the marshal's supper she leaned, jerked her head sideways and said, 'Get them out of here before they get into a fight.'

Rowe recognized the rangemen, they rode for B A. Except for the arguers Alice's other patrons concentrated on eating. Rowe knew old Barton; by nature he was argumentative but not genuinely belligerent. Both the stockmen were younger, work-hardened individuals. Rowe knew them by sight.

Neither of them had ever been genuinely troublesome in town.

He asked Alice to make up a canister of stew with a side order of black coffee.

When the other diners heard that order given the café got quiet. The town marshal only asked for extra food when he had a prisoner over at the jailhouse.

There were other ways to attract and hold the attention in the café, but for Rowe to want food for a prisoner when the rumour of a stage robbery was circulating meant he had a highwayman in his jail cell.

Two diners paid up and departed. The third man to leave the counter to depart was Jackson Barton and he paused behind the marshal to brush Rowe's shoulder as he leaned to speak. 'Who you got this time, Marshal. Someone stop a stage?'

Alice was carrying empty plates to her kitchen. She wasn't the only one who seemed not to be awaiting the marshal's reply.

Rowe did not look around when he answered the liveryman.

'Something like that, Jack.'

Several diners departed, the last man to go had hardly touched his meal. The café became as quiet as a cemetery.

When Alice came from her kitchen carrying two dented tin containers that resembled army mess kits and placed them in front of Rowe he had only half finished his meal. He arose and under several watchful diners put silver coins beside his plate, smiled and left the eatery carrying the tin canisters. Alice's remaining diners went from the counter to the roadway window where they could see the lawman cross over and disappear inside his jailhouse.

He barred the roadway door from the inside, took the food to his prisoner and without a word went back to his office to sit at the table, roll a smoke and wait.

Because the livery barn was at the southerly end of town and the Blue Duck Saloon was closer to the centre of Fleming, old Barton did his chores before heading up yonder to repeat what the marshal had said, by which time the two rangemen from the café had reached the saloon where they had downed two jolts of pop skull as they repeated to the saloon's steadies that a stage had been robbed and the highwayman was in Rowe Harmon's jailhouse.

One man, sharp-featured and balding took exception. His name was Les Welsh. He was boss of the stage-company's corralyard at the upper north end of town. He glared at the speaker from Alice's café.

'That's a damned lie. Hasn't been one of my stages robbed in more'n three years. Wherever in hell did you hear that cock'n bull yarn?'

An old man playing matchstick poker with three other old men twisted in his chair by the roadway window. 'How do you know, Les? There's still coaches comin' from up north.'

The stager stamped out of the saloon heading for his corralyard. For a fact the southbound late-day coach hadn't arrived. It wasn't due for another hour or such a matter.

The Blue Duck's other customers drifted away to go around town with the news. Nothing like a stage robbery had happened in a long while. In fact, nothing that could capture folk's interest had happened. Fleming had been working itself up for several weeks in anticipation of the B A cattle drive. This particular bit of gossip would spread like wildfire; it would take precedent over the cattle drive arriving at the north end of town tomorrow.

Rowe Harmon was asleep at his table in the jail-house when a small crowd arrived to rattle his roadway door.

He had reason to be upset when the visitors pushed their way inside wanting to see Rowe's highwayman. They wanted to know how he had made the capture.

Rowe got rid of them with heartfelt profanity and was back at the table when Alice arrived. He waited until she had explained what had caused the uproar then told her he had gone up yonder, something she had encouraged him to do, and had captured a man up there carrying a running iron in his shirt pocket.

They visited for a solid hour. When he mentioned Chris Humes, Alice reminded him that he'd been in the café when both men had invited her to go buggy riding with them and that she had gone with Rowe. She also said Humes had been trying to court her.

When Rowe stood up she said, 'I never encouraged him.'

Rowe was reaching for his hat when he said, 'Where does he stay?'

Alice also arose. 'I have no idea. He shows up every day at the café.' She was at the door when she said, 'Is the man you locked up the stage robber?'

Rowe answered curtly. 'Do you know for a fact a stage was stopped?'

She shook her head. The corralyard boss hadn't been in her café since he'd made a crude remark and she'd told him to leave and not come back.

After she left, Rowe walked the full distance to the corralyard where the short-tempered boss was helping remove harness from four tired animals. He acknowledged the marshal's presence by ordering two yard men to take over and jerked his head for Rowe to follow him to his littered little office with its powerful cigar scent.

Rowe asked if the stage he was helping to get unhitched was from up north and Welsh answered around a cigar stub he was lighting.

'That's it. The last coach until in the morning an' if you asked that because it was supposed to've been robbed, the answer is — no! It wasn't robbed! I got no idea where that story started, but I can tell you for a damned fact I ain't had a robbery in three, four years.'

As the yard boss killed the match and heartily puffed up a respectable cloud of smoke he sat down at a cluttered desk. 'Who you got locked up? Or, have you got anyone locked up? Rowe, I been in this town seven years; before that I was up at Laramie, an' before that down near Amarillo an' I can tell you on a stack of Bibles I never before been in a place as infested with gossips in my whole damned life, an' it ain't just the womenfolk. That old unwashed goat who's got the livery . . . him'n his friends was borned with tongues that's hinged in the middle an' flap at both ends. You care for a cigar, Marshal?'

Rowe declined the offer, left the office, crossed over to the Blue Duck and asked more questions. He was assured by several Blue Duck steadies that not only had a stage been stopped but was carrying a bullion box which the highwayman rode off with.

He was heading for the jailhouse when Jake Hersheimer intercepted him out front of the general store.

Hersheimer was neither tall nor young. He had an elegant fringe of hair completely around a hairless top. He was an affable, excitable and high-strung individual. He also wanted to know about the marshal's prisoner.

Rowe tried to escape by telling the storekeeper his prisoner hadn't robbed any stage that he knew of and suggested that Hersheimer go up yonder and talk to Les Welsh.

Hersheimer fidgeted. He wasn't the only person who avoided the corralyard boss if he possibly could.

As Rowe was turning away, Hersheimer said, 'You'll be in town tomorrow, I expect.'

Rowe showed a humourless small

smile. 'I'll be here, Jake. Burke Arnold's riders don't get troublesome, but if you're worryin' keep the store locked until the drive's gone past.'

It was good advice, probably unnecessary, but valid, and Hersheimer said he would lock up. He needed a day off anyway, it was getting along in the year for fishing the mountain lakes, his hobby, but whether he caught anything or not he'd be out of town.

He called after the marshal, 'I'd take it kindly, Mr Harmon, if you'd sort of mind the store. I'm going fishing tomorrow.'

Rowe visited Bryan Cullom in his cell room. He wanted to know where he might find Chris Humes. The answer he got came with a sour grin.

'Under a rock, Marshal. Maybe in Montana by now. Or Idaho. What makes you think I'd know where the bastard is?'

'Because he's here in Fleming.'

'Did you try the roomin'-house? Or maybe the hay loft at the livery barn? I got no idea an' that's the truth. If I was to guess I'd say figure out why he's here an' go from there.'

Rowe returned to his office. He was half of an opinion why Humes would be in town. He went over to the eatery. Alice said Humes hadn't been back. She had a feeling he wouldn't be back.

'Maybe he knows you're looking for him, Rowe.'

He had already speculated about that. How Humes would know the law was looking for him would be anyone's guess.

He asked Alice to hang a sheet in the café's roadway window if he showed up, and returned to the roadway just in time to meet the B A range boss who had come to town to make sure folks were prepared for the drive through town some time after sun-up the following morning.

Davidson was interested to the extent of wanting to know if the marshal had gone up yonder looking for the log house with the dead man in it.

Rowe's reply was ruefully given. 'I went up there. The house smelled like a tanyard. I brought back a feller carryin' a cinch ring runnin' iron.'

'What's his name?'

'Up there he said it was Joe Smith. Down here in my jail cell it's Bryan Cullom.'

The range boss shook his head. 'Never heard of him. You brought him in for carryin' a cinch ring runnin' iron?'

'It's all I could think of. It's not much, but now I got him down here I got to keep you'n Burke Arnold from wantin' his hide. By the way, there was three of 'em. One's buried up there. His name was Jack Ballow. I got Cullom an' I want to find the one named Humes. He's still around.'

'Here? In Fleming?' Davidson asked with narrowed eyes. 'Mister Arnold'll like to know that. Where is he?'

Rowe audibly sighed. 'I been lookin'.'

'I'll go tell the boss. He'll want to come back with the lads to help find the son of a bitch.'

Rowe very emphatically shook his head. 'Don't you tell Burke what I told you. Maybe I'd better lock you up. Burke'll ride in here loaded for bear. Josh, there's enough upset folks about cattle bein' drove through town. You get Burke fired up an' there'll be a damned war. I think you better come with me.'

The range boss took a fighting stance. He wasn't a match for the marshal, but his stance and expression hinted that he might be willing to put that to a test.

The marshal smiled. 'Give me your word you won't mention anythin'.'

The range boss loosened visibly and nodded but he did not smile. He volunteered to help find Chris Humes and got a negative head shake from the marshal. 'I got a reason for wantin' to find him by myself.'

The range boss departed looking glum. He hadn't been gone long before the Blue Duck's proprietor, a stocky, swarthy man named Pete Orni walked in. It was said locally that he was some kind of Indian, or maybe Mexican. He was Italian, and had never bothered to clear up that question.

He sank down on the wall bench and sighed like someone who had just lost his best friend. Eventually he said, 'That danged preacher. I wish he'd stick to harness-makin'. He's trying to work up the women-folk to meet Arnold's drive when it's ready to enter town an' cause a stampede by wavin' their aprons an' whatnot.'

Rowe leaned back from his table. 'Where'd you hear that?'

'From one of them old men who just about lives at the saloon.' Pete Orni blew out a breath of air. 'You ever hear of anythin' more ridiculous in your life?'

'What's his idea? That drive's dang near a holiday an' has been since long before I came here.' The marshal arose. 'I'll go talk to the preacher.'

The Blue Duck's owner also arose. 'Won't do any good. Preachers get

77

somethin' fixed in their heads you can't get it out with dynamite. I know. Where I was raised priests used to come around an' tell my folks I had the Devil's mark on me. They wouldn't let me out of the house for a week except to go to church where they'd get down on their knees an' beg Gawd to get rid of the Devil's mark. For two solid hours. When I was older, the priest got transferred. I wanted to catch him alone but it never happened.'

Rowe waited out the swarthy man's lamentation before asking a question. 'You know a feller named Humes?'

'I know him. Haven't seen him lately. Why?'

'I want to find him.'

Pete Orni got as far as the door before asking his own question. 'They want to hang that highwayman you got locked up. Just about everyone who's been in wants to, but I expect you know that. Are you ready an' waitin'?'

Rowe nodded. What he didn't know for a fact he could safely surmise. 'My

78

prisoner didn't rob a stage. No one did. Go talk to Les at the corralyard. None of his rigs's been stopped.'

The saloonman departed. His expression had not brightened at what the marshal had said about his prisoner. Once the nervous folks in Fleming got their minds made up, reasoning or facts wouldn't change them and Rowe knew it.

He got two of those canisters from Alice for his prisoner, not because he had a humanitarian feeling, but because the prisoner was the only person he knew who could answer questions about the other cattle thieves, one in particular.

But the prisoner emptied the canister as though he hadn't eaten in weeks and consistently shook his head when Rowe asked questions until he had washed everything down by draining the tin of coffee, and belched.

Then he said, 'In my time I've run across all kinds, but, Chris, for all he's done an' if it's only half true, he's never went to prison, an' that's one hell of an accomplishment.'

That scrap of information, true or not, only indifferently interested Fleming's marshal. He gave Cullom another sack of the makings and took the tins back to Alice.

The eatery was empty. She was finishing at cleaning up and offered Rowe a cup of new coffee. As she was filling a cup she said, 'On the house. Have you found Humes?'

He thanked her for the coffee, drank the cup down, pushed the cup aside and reached for the makings. The pocket was empty. Alice dug in a drawer, produced half a sack an absent-minded diner had left, waited until Rowe had lighted up then asked again if he'd found Humes. When he shook his head she offered to refill his cup and when he put his palm over the cup she said, 'Funny thing about him. He drinks coffee, but he got me to brew tea several times. When I did it he said his mother made the best tea he ever tasted.'

Rowe nodded as indifferently as he'd done over at the jailhouse when his prisoner had told him for all his lifetime of robbing and shooting Humes had never been in prison.

He asked if she'd heard the folks against B A's drive through town were going to try and stampede the herd with aprons and whatnot.

Alice smiled. 'The minister asked me to join. He said half the womenfolk had agreed to do it.' Alice's smile faded. 'He should have talked to the menfolk. They'd never let their womenfolk do such a thing. Besides . . . Do you know Josh Davidson? He'll be up front. He'll scatter them like chickens.'

Rowe arose from the counter, would have put a silver coin beside the cup but Alice's scowl changed his mind. As he was leaving she said, 'The store'll be closed. Rowe . . . ?'

'What?'

'The women are right. After the cattle pass through, a person has to

81

watch their step in the road for days.'

Outside, Fleming seemed deserted. People with dogs would be chaining them. Nothing caused more havoc among driven cattle than loose dogs.

A battered old wagon passed the northward buildings at a plodding walk. Someone had sometime branded the sideboards with B A's mark about three times normal size. Rowe watched the driver begin to angle toward the front of Hersheimer's general store. He wasn't exactly surprised but he leaned on an overhang post to watch. Always before the B A wagon came in the drag, after the cattle had passed through.

He leaned to kill his smoke as a man came up, stopped to also watch the wagon and spoke. 'It'll be the last time.'

Rowe looked up and around. The harness-making preacher was watching the wagon. 'They should've forbidden it years ago. Who does Burke Arnold think he is, anyway?' When Rowe didn't answer, his companion faced around with the expression of someone who had just been blessed with an inspiration.

'Marshal, you can arrest him. He's got no right to drive cattle directly through town. There's plenty of territory on both sides, east and west for miles.' When Rowe fixed his attention on the approaching wagon the irate preacher said, 'Marshal!'

Rowe answered brusquely. 'That's up to the town council.'

'Is it?' the preacher retorted. 'You're the law. You've arrested folks for other things without getting the council's permission in advance. I've seen you do it.'

Rowe saw the wagon's driver raise an arm to a couple of old men out front of the Blue Duck who waved back.

'Marshal, no other town I've been in would allow this.'

Rowe straightened up off the post he'd been leaning on. 'You been here three years, Ben. You've seen this happen three times. By now you'd ought to know the schoolmarm even closes up so's the kids can wave an' holler to the riders. It's sort of a holiday, like Mr Lincoln's birthday. You want some advice? Tell those women-folk you've fired up to stampede the cattle to stay inside. Don't wave blankets or whatever they got. If they make a stampede there's goin' to be some downright irate husbands an' they'll look you up too. Hell, it only lasts maybe half an hour.'

'It's what's left behind, Marshal.'

Rowe nodded to the pair of range-men with the wagon. They nodded back and one man leaned over the side to jettison an overworked cud. The preacher also nodded, but that com-monplace indication of civility was not matched by the bleak expression on his face.

Someone pushed a heavy door wide open as the wagon stopped in front of Hersheimer's store. Rowe heard one of the wagoneers call a greeting which Jake Hersheimer returned.

The man standing with Rowe scornfully said, 'Whiskey drinkers. It goes with their trade.'

Rowe agreed. 'It's also good for snakebite an' the summer complaint. Ben, an old uncle of mine who got hurt pretty bad in the war said whiskey helped ease a man's pain. He said if whiskey didn't have a reason the Lord wouldn't have fixed things so's folks could make it . . . Ben?'

The younger man was turning to leave when he answered. 'I met a man north of town who was putting together his supper. He invited me to join him.'

'Did you?'

'No. I drink coffee. He didn't have any. By the looks of him I thought he was maybe a rangeman. He was the first rangeman I ever saw who drank tea.'

Rowe stiffened a little where he stood. 'Did he say his name?

'No. I was on my way back here and I wanted to get home early.'

'Was he leading a pack horse?'

'As a matter of fact he was. Rode one and led the other one.'

'Did he say where he was going?'

'He didn't say and I didn't ask. I wanted to get back before sundown.'

5

In the Saddle!

Rowe went down to the livery barn. Jack Barton was in a friendly mood. He'd hired the town's dimwit at two bits a day to do chores which meant Barton could now spend more time among cronies at the Blue Duck.

Rowe herded Barton into his smelly little combination office and harness-room.

Barton sat on an ancient stool that had one short leg and looked enquiringly at the marshal.

Rowe said, 'That feller whose gatherings you went through — is he still around?'

Barton shook his head. 'I'll say one thing for him. He left two dollars on my table. He lit out yestiddy some time. His animals and pack was gone when I got back from Pete's place. Why? Did he skip out owin' money?'

Rowe ignored the question. 'While he was around did he mention where he was goin', or where he'd been, or anythin' like that?'

Old Barton got a worried look on his face. 'We didn't talk much. He hung around Pete's saloon an' Alice Gordon's eatery. Maybe one of them could answer your questions. Like I said, he left a pair of greenbacks on this here table which was about what he owed me for puttin' up his animals. When a man's that honest . . . hell, he could've just rigged out and left. I got to say honest folks don't do business with me very often. Marshal . . . ?'

Rowe paused in the doorway to say, 'Thanks, Jack,' before returning to the roadway.

He crossed the road and hiked northerly toward the Blue Duck and was intercepted by a sturdy built, greying woman with a jaw square enough to use for a wedge in splitting logs. Her name was Ann Butler, she was the local blacksmith's wife. She barred Rowe's northward progress with both hands on her hips.

'Marshal, we're fixin' to stop Burke Arnold from drivin' any more cattle through this town. You'll want to stay out of it. We'll gather at the north end of town before sun-up in the mornin'. If you haven't been invited to interfere I'm tellin' you right now — don't.'

Rowe looked past, saw two hungry men rattle Alice's door before answering the blacksmith's wife. 'Ann, don't meddle. You stampede Arnold's drive an' there'll be hell to pay.'

'I expect there will,' the woman replied. 'If you was any kind of a lawman you'd ride up there right now an' make Mr Arnold go out an' around town. Every year there's flies by the hunnert an' a person's got to wear high boots to cross the road. Preacher Ben's goin' to take this up with the town council. My husband sits on it. I can tell you for a fact he's goin' to vote against it, somethin' that lily-livered bunch should've done years ago.'

Rowe considered the woman. He knew her very well. She was one of those human beings who carried unpopular banners. She and the marshal had locked horns on other matters, mostly of less consequence than the present one.

He forced a small smile as he said, 'Ann, do us all a favour, leave it be.'

With fisted hands at her sides she glared. 'I told my husband when they figured to hire you what our town needed was not a talker, but a doer. You're goin' to take sides with old Arnold an' that'll be the biggest mistake of your life!'

Rowe held his small smile as he watched the blacksmith's wife go storming across the road where she turned north in the direction of the church and its adjoining parsonage.

He saw the pair of hungry townsmen turn away from the café, going in the direction of the Blue Duck.

The confrontation with Ann Butler didn't upset him, but it made him aware of something that required a decision. If he saddled up and went in search of the tea-drinker he would probably be unable to overtake the fugitive and return with him today.

No one travelling with a pack animal could make as good time as someone travelling without one. It would help his pursuit if Humes had no reason to travel fast, but the day was wearing along and if the preacher had met Humes yesterday along toward late afternoon, to make up lost time Rowe would have to be gone from town at the very least until tomorrow, late, by which time there would be turmoil in Fleming; the irate women would have caused it and the local law would be miles away.

His choice was between two evils: ride down Chris Humes or stay in town to prevent a variety of trouble that would create outraged animosity for years.

He went over to the jailhouse and brought his prisoner to the office, told him where to sit and got comfortable behind the table that had served Fleming's lawmen for thirty years.

His prisoner was hungry. Justified or not, Rowe ignored complaints to ask questions.

'How long had you three been partnered up?'

'About a year. Maybe a tad longer. Long enough to build that log house, the shed an' the corral.'

Rowe nodded. 'Long enough to get your rustlin' business started up.'

Cullom ignored that. 'You got the makings?'

Rowe fished them from a pocket as he said, 'You run out?'

The prisoner nodded as he caught the little sack. 'Run out yestiddy.'

'How about Humes?'

'He uses snuff.'

'In a year together you fellers got to know each other pretty well. Where did he come from?'

'Texas, mostly, but he was over as far as Idaho.'

'Worked cattle did he?'

'He done that a-plenty. He was as good a roper as I ever saw.'

'Fellers sittin' around winter nights get to talkin'.'

Bryan Cullom inhaled and exhaled before saying, 'Me'n Jack was gettin' awful tired of him talkin' about his women.'

'He talked of other things, Bryan.'

'He did, but if we shot the bull around the stove for long he'd get back to women.'

'What were the other things he talked about?'

Cullom flicked ash and craftily smiled. 'Marshal, I already told you. I know what you're doin', but I got no idea where he'd go. Just one thing: he'd marry 'em. That was funny the first four or five times he talked about it. After that it was just plain tiresome.'

'If he went north would there be a woman up there?'

'More'n one, Marshal. He was married to a storekeeper's daughter up near Lodgepole in Montana. Before he had to go that far he told us about marryin' a widow-woman who owned a spread. He couldn't joke about that one. She run somethin' like six, eight hunnert cows. Hired him on. She already had four riders.'

'What town, Bryan?'

The crafty grin resurfaced. 'Well now, Marshal, I just plain can't remember.'

Rowe dug out his bottle of whiskey, downed two swallows and held the bottle looking straight at his prisoner.

Cullom took down a deep drag from his quirly, flicked ash again although there wasn't enough to shake loose and stopped grinning. He leaned and held out his left hand.

Bryan pushed the bottle halfway. 'What town?'

'Custer, over in West Wyoming.'

Rowe released his grip on the bottle, leaned back and watched Cullom swallow three times then took back the bottle.

As he was punching in the cork he said, 'Where in hell is Custer, Wyoming?'

His prisoner was in the initial glow and this time the smile was genuine. 'I got no idea. I was in Wyoming just once. At Fort Laramie with winter settin' in. I got out of there an' never stopped until I was down in New Messico's border country where they don't know what snow is.'

Cullom killed his cigarette and leaned to leave the bench. 'Marshal, did you ever starve a prisoner to death?'

As Rowe went to hold the cell-room door open he drily said, 'No, but there's always a first time.'

He locked Cullom in the cell and made a parting statement. 'All right, I'll go get you something to eat.'

Cullom smiled genuinely for the second time. 'You wouldn't want to leave me that bottle would you?'

Rowe returned to his office without

answering, reset his hat, locked up from out front and crossed over heading for Alice's eatery.

There was a man outside trying to peek through the roadway window. He was the 'breed Indian who doctored animals, mostly dogs and horses around the Fleming countryside. He was old, lined and friendly. His name was Abe White. He wasn't white, he was a tad lighter than a sun-dried adobe brick. His full name was Abraham White Tail. For obvious reasons he did not use his full name. He was a friendly individual and there was no denying, he had a gift for healing and curing.

When the marshal came up he turned wearing an ingratiating smile and said, 'Not in there. I been waitin' for her to unlock the door since noon. Maybe she's taken sick. She's got a livin'-room off the back, don't she?'

Rowe had only an idea where Alice lived; for all their playful courting he had never been beyond the counter of her café nor had she ever visited him at the rooming-house.

He rattled the door, leaned to look inside from the same window and straightened back as the old bronco said, 'She was here earlier. I got an early breakfast. She seemed all right then.'

Rowe left Abe White, turned down the nearest dog trot and emerged in the eastside alley. There was a locked door which gave access from the built-on lean-to where Alice lived to the alley. He rattled that door too, and would have peered through a window if there had been one.

When he returned back the way he had gone the old 'breed had been joined by three other patrons, one of whom sulkily said they'd go eat at Fleming's only other café, operated by the old widow-woman who, despite her age and having once had a husband for whom she had made meals, had no talent for cooking.

The old 'breed lingered, the hungry individuals abandoned the hope of being decently fed and departed. They went up to the Blue Duck; whiskey was no substitute for a cooked meal but for a fact it dulled the pangs of hunger.

Rowe and Abe White commiserated until the old 'breed also departed. He wasn't the only 'breed in the Fleming countryside. There were also several families of full bloods. No one who was hungry went long without a meal, particularly if he was as respected as old Abe White was.

Rowe didn't begin to really worry until he had gone to Hersheimer's, after visiting the other café, where the pithy proprietor replied to his questions about Alice with a disagreeable snort.

He began to seriously worry after he went up to the saloon where the patrons of the Blue Duck unanimously complained; they were mostly the unattached men, widowers or single individuals.

Pete Orni complained too. All he'd heard since midday was about the café being closed. No one appeared upset beyond the fact that the café was locked up. The easiest speculation had to do with illness, but that possibility didn't ameliorate the marshal's increasing anxiety.

He returned to the café. Nothing had changed, the roadway door was locked. He returned to the alley, climbed the two low stairs and knocked and rattled the door. A foraging dog stood beyond a stone's distance eyeing him. He leaned on the door. The dog offered friendship with a wag of its tail. The marshal let the dog come close enough to have his back scratched. He wasn't a tall dog so Rowe had to lean. His scratching was only momentarily vigorous.

He had missed it before when he and the 'breed had been back here; several feet beyond the dog were tracks coming from the south and going northward with signs that the horse had lingered.

Rowe straightened up slowly following the tracks by sight. When they continued northward each impression was deeper. *The horse was only shod in front.*

Rowe made a smoke and lighted it. As he moved away from the building the dog ducked through a wooden fence with missing slats and disappeared.

Rowe followed the tracks until they eventually passed behind the saloon. He paused, scanning ahead. The tracks veered slightly and were lost in the distance where they left town paralleling the stage road but easterly.

He went ahead until he was certain and turned back. He could have returned to the front roadway, but he walked the distance by way of the alley until he reached the unfenced cast-off yard behind the smithy before crossing over to the livery barn.

Jack Barton was not around. The friendly youth he had hired was out back washing horses and smiled widely when he saw the marshal.

Rowe didn't return the smile, but he nodded, went to catch his grulla, took him inside to be rigged out and led him up as far as the jailhouse where he ignored the shouts of his prisoner, took saddle-bags, his booted Winchester and returned to the horse.

He rode north under considerable wide-eyed scrutiny. When he was no longer in sight the Blue Duck's steadies went back inside where one of them said, 'You see his face? He's goin' to hunt up Burke Arnold an' my guess is that there won't be no B A cattle drove through town tomorrow.'

It wasn't true, but with Fleming in a state of high tension about Burke Arnold's drive through town it raised the hopes among the opposition but was not believed by those in favour.

Locating the tracks was not difficult for the marshal. There was other sign. The closer he got to the holding ground of the Arnold herd the more tracks interfered, but Rowe had daylight and time. He made slow progress for about a mile and had one encounter that stopped him in his tracks.

Josh Davidson had been busy since daybreak keeping restless animals from drifting. Where he and the marshal met was far enough north-easterly for the range boss to be turning back.

Davidson dismounted as he greeted the lawman and lifted his hat to mop off sweat and show a rueful smile as he said, 'You keepin' track of us? Cutbacks don't go south they go north.'

Rowe didn't dismount, but he let his reins sag. 'I'm not worryin' about the cattle,' he said. 'Look there; you see those tracks?'

The range boss squinted, walked a yard or so and wagged his head. 'You lookin' for someone who only shoes his horse in front?'

Rowe nodded, snugged up the reins a little, nodded again and continued riding.

The range boss followed Rowe with his eyes. He told his horse the marshal didn't act like they'd been friends for many years. Josh Davidson had been so busy keeping the strays in check, plus a

102

number of days had gone by since he had mentioned seeing those tracks to the marshal; it failed to register. As he swung up he said, 'Rowe's got the belly complaint more'n likely.'

The sign was easier to follow once Rowe got far enough along to be travelling open country.

He rode steadily without haste. As much of a lead as the rider he wanted already had, the horse hadn't been born that could close the gap.

With the eventual arrival of early dusk the tracking was easy as long as enough daylight lingered. Rowe knew the country ahead for a hundred miles. He was figuring places Humes might stop. There was a village due north, about half the size of Fleming. The tracks appeared to be heading in that direction right up to the point where Rowe came to a busy creek known locally as Custer's Creek.

Whether it had been named for *the* Custer was anyone's guess. For a fact he had been in this part of the country years back.

It didn't matter nor did Rowe ponder long. The tracks went down into the water and did not emerge on the far side.

Rowe reined to a stop looking both ways. Somewhere the oddly shod horse had come out. If he left the creek down south somewhere he'd eventually be back in Fleming country and it was turning sundown by the hour.

Rowe paralleled the creek northward, rode about two miles and did not find where Humes had come out of the water.

He topped out over a long-spending north-south rib of land and halted. He was no longer watching for Humes, he was watching for movement, preferably of a mounted rider.

There was nothing moving in any direction. He returned to the creek anxious about wasting time.

He was considering pushing ahead as far as that hamlet when he saw something that stopped him in his tracks.

By fading light they were not distinguishable from the saddle so he dismounted and led his horse.

A horse who left only shod tracks in front had left the creek on the west side where underbrush and willows were thicker than the hair on a dog's back.

He had to lead off bending slightly over. Nor did he satisfy himself whose sign he was reading for a fair distance; not until the clinging mud and water were left behind.

He stopped where the tracks were abundantly clear and built a smoke which he lighted inside his hat, killed the fire and said, 'Son of a bitch!'

The tracks were going south. On the far side of the creek and far enough northward to have discouraged some trackers but not all of them. Particularly not Rowe Harmon whose reason to hunt Humes down was as valid as anyone's motivation could be.

Humes had ridden beside the creek for willow shelter until he arrived where someone had thinned the underbrush for some reason that for the moment wasn't important, then he only rode with the creek for a few hundred yards before veering westerly. He left sign going south but on a westward angle.

If he went far enough in that westerly direction he was going to encounter forested uplands where mammoth over-ripe trees made progress difficult; in some places downright impossible for someone on horseback.

When full dark arrived, Rowe continued, but on a loose rein. He was assuming Humes was not going to alter course again, definitely a chancy thing to do, but he wanted to find Humes before he settled for the night, less for the sake of locating his man than because he wanted to do the overtaking before the passenger riding behind Humes's cantle had to spend the night with the fugitive.

He was sweating hard. Some of that was caused after he had to dismount and lead his mount. The ground was rocky and uneven. In places he could only barely make out the tracks.

If he was tired he did not notice it, but his horse was tiring and hungry. He frequently yanked hard to get enough slack to duck his head and snatch something to eat.

The closer they got to the foremost fringe of timber the less grass and browse was available. That was when the grulla fought the bit hardest.

Rowe was slowed by boulders, some man-sized. He avoided the largest ones but stumbled often over the smaller ones.

When a three-quarter moon arrived its light helped but not enough. Rowe wanted to hasten. Once he tried it by simply ignoring the ground. When he lost the sign he had to waste more time by back-tracking until he found it.

He was favoured by a cloudless sky,

but didn't consider that until he relived the pursuit weeks later.

There was a point where the tired man stumbled more than he avoided stumbling. The moon was high. Its ghostly light seemed stronger. Rowe stopped once when the horse became particularly insistent. He would need the animal somewhere ahead so he sank down on a rotten old deadfall log and let the grulla drag its reins as it voraciously grazed.

Rowe considered where he was. It surprised him to be following along the base of the heavily forested highlands with which he was familiar.

If he could have drawn a straight easterly line the far end would reach the westernmost area of Fleming.

He snugged up the cinch, mounted and afterward only occasionally dismounted to read sign.

Humes had left sign enough to throw some practised trackers off. In fact, back at Custer Creek most sign readers would have given up.

They didn't have Rowe's motivating urgency.

Humes was heading for the highlands clearing where the log house was situated!

6

Two Hostages!

Rowe lighted up another smoke inside his hat so the brief spark of flame would not be visible. He had the night-blackened heavily timbered country on his right side. Eventually he would ride among the trees. He wanted to cover ground rapidly which he could not do if he left the lowland border country.

If he was guessing wrong, if Humes and his hostage were not at the log-house clearing he was reconciled to abandoning the hunt until daybreak. Perhaps abandoning it altogether. His horse was dragging its hind feet.

He was paralleling the route he had taken when he'd left town while there had been daylight. This only passingly concerned him. What troubled him most was Humes leaving a trail which might have got him far enough northward to be beyond reach. He tried to imagine reasons for Humes's elaborate ruse, if his real intention had been the log-house clearing.

What put an end to his speculation was the nearby scream of a mountain lion.

His weary horse jumped so high Rowe had to grab the horn to stay on top.

The horse lit down fighting the bit. He was poised to run and the best Rowe could accomplish was to bend the grulla's head so far around the horse could not run. It stumbled, nearly fell and Rowe gave it enough slack to prevent this. Some horses would have fought with all their strength. Not even a bear inspired as much terror in horses as mountain lions did.

Rowe got the grulla facing easterly and let him have his head for a fair distance before he could get him down to a lope and about a half-mile further along he managed to get him down to a

111

walk. It was a springy gait: If the cougar had howled again the grulla would have broken into belly-down flight.

When the struggle ended, Rowe was a long mile south in open country. He turned back, angling south-westerly so that when he could see the uplands he would be at least another mile south-ward.

The horse was walking on eggs. The tiredness would return but not for some time. The fact that mountain lions were not night hunters encouraged Rowe to wonder if it hadn't been a female lion with cubs who had caught horse scent and although a horse posed no threat, if cubs were involved . . .

Rowe finally saw the uplands with their huge old trees as closely spaced as soldiers. He had to guess when it was time to go up there. It would be slow going but eventually he would be in familiar territory.

The horse offered only a little resistance when he was reined uphill. The reason became obvious when

Rowe heard water breaking over rocks. The horse hadn't had a drink since Custer Creek and that had been when there had still been daylight.

Judging by the trampled surroundings the watercourse had to be the only place animals drank for some distance. The grulla tanked up, stood patiently to be re-bitted and left the water with less reluctance than resignation. He had covered a lot of miles since yesterday and while his kind, like true buckskins were noted for endurance, there were limits.

Rowe might have dozed in the saddle if all his attention wasn't required to make a zigzag path among the trees. It was where he had to back track a yard or so to get clear that he heard something. When he was working ahead past an ancient burn he drew rein to listen.

If there actually had been a sound it was not repeated. He relied more on his horse than on himself for detection.

It was a good policy. The grulla was

passing out of the burn and was re-entering the dark forest when it threw up its head and stumbled.

Rowe stopped, waited briefly before dismounting to lead the horse. He had to be close to his destination. The difficulty with heavily timbered country was that any approach but one marked by usage was likely to lead nowhere.

They were going up and around a huge old deadfall when the stillness was broken, this time with a sound Rowe and his mount simultaneously recognized. It was the same sound that had stopped him the last time he was up here; the unmistakable call of a horse.

Rowe waited. There was no repetition. He gave his horse its head and walked beside it.

The horse did not falter although he sashayed to avoid colliding with trees.

Rowe's second cause for interest was the smell of woodsmoke. It would serve him as a guide. There was no wind, there rarely was in thickly timbered country. He did not rely on his horse but picked his route carefully keeping the scent strongest dead ahead.

The grulla abruptly set back, planted all four feet down hard, raised its head and before Rowe could clamp it over the nostrils, whinnied for all he was worth.

The answer was almost immediate and it came from a slightly more south-easterly direction.

Rowe called his horse a name that would have caused a fight if the animal'd had two legs instead of four and jerked the reins.

The grulla was a hackamore-broke horse. Even after quite a few years of responding to steel bits it responded promptly. In fact it would have walked ahead if Rowe hadn't growled and hauled back.

The smoke scent was strong the next time they stopped. Rowe couldn't see the log house but where he stopped was at the westernmost edge of the clearing where it had been cleared of timber around the house.

What held him motionless was something he could neither explain or had anticipated. Where there was supposed to be two horses in the clearing, there were three.

They were as still as statues, heads up, ears pointing in his direction. This time it wasn't scent that intrigued them, it was a sighting.

Rowe's surprise didn't interfere with his sense of caution. He picked a way southerly passing deeper into the forest. Each time he edged closer he could see the three horses. They were still looking in the direction where they had last seen the two-legged creature with its four-legged companion.

He warily continued southward, occasionally sidetracking to watch the house. If there was a light it would not be visible from the rear. When the three partners had built the house they had provided only the front wall with a window.

As long as he was behind the house or even if he got where he could see the south wall he would be unable to see if there was a light burning.

Where he could see along the south wall the timber had been cleared as far as a trail leading away from the clearing. Without being aware of it that trail was the one Bryan Cullom had used going south to the canyon where he'd burnt the Sword C mark on Burke Arnold's B A cow.

He and his companions had used the trail when they left the clearing to get supplies. It was sufficiently worn to indicate use but beyond that it served only a minimal purpose.

Rowe stopped to tie his horse, he didn't like leaving the horse but he hadn't ridden all those hours to be delayed in his manhunt now.

He took the saddle gun with him and used every advantage to prowl easterly past the trail into an uninter-rupted stand of timber which made it possible for him to get far enough eastward to the place where a fir split and a stump made it possible to see the cabin's front.

There was light showing from the only window and where it was possible to see it, there was a spindrift of smoke arising from the chimney.

He was in the exact place where Bryan Cullom had caught him from behind. He wanted a smoke and was as hungry as a bitch wolf. Earlier he had also been tired, which he no longer was.

There were a number of ways he might be able to get Humes out of the house and every one of them involved letting the fugitive know he — someone — was out in the night.

The moon had been slanting away for some time which he hadn't noticed and didn't heed now. If he hadn't come up here alone . . . but he had. That third horse bothered him. Whoever that animal belonged to, it hadn't been ridden by Humes's partners of whom one was dead and the other was locked in the Fleming jailhouse.

Who the person was provided room

for endless speculation. If Rowe managed to be over there where the light showed, it would double his risk.

He left the split hiking on around almost as far as the place where he'd left his horse tethered on his previous visit.

He rolled and lighted a cigarette. As long as the men — and the woman — remained inside they would not detect tobacco smoke, but the longer Rowe pondered the more time was being wasted.

He had to either get inside or get those over yonder to come outside. And it was getting cold which meant the night was wearing along toward dawn. After daylight arrived his chance of detection would increase.

He started back around the way he had come with some idea in mind of decreasing the odds by rousting the three horses in the clearing, get them fleeing in any direction but westerly, in general the way he had used to get where he now was.

After daylight there was an excellent possibility that the routed horses might go westerly as far as the stage road and be caught by someone down there.

Jack Barton would recognize two of them, the one Humes rode and the one he led.

When he was far enough to reach the place where the horses in the meadow had first seen him he stood beside a huge old weather-worn fir where he had a good sighting of the three horses. It wasn't light enough to discern saddle marks. He risked sidling closer, but still could not see what he was looking for. The last time he moved he was risking detection but if the men inside hadn't come out earlier there was reason to hope they wouldn't do it now.

The horses weren't facing him and as they grazed along their ribs were invisible on both sides.

He gave it up, went back where the grulla was dozing, led it through timber into a smaller opening, removed the bridle, loosened the cinch and watched it graze while he considered ways of attracting at least one of the men in the log house to come out.

Sooner or later they would have to leave the house. He found a place where he had an upward view of sky. The moon was not up there. His best calculation placed the time to be somewhere close to dawn's first light. He moved closer to the scant place where his horse was standing hip shot with its eyes closed. He was about thirty feet away when the animal opened his eyes and turned his head.

Rowe spoke soothingly. The horse squared partly around until they were facing each other. Rowe had the impression the grulla wasn't looking straight at him. He continued to use the technique known as 'chumming' until he could touch the horse's neck, not to pat it, to stroke it. The horse did not move. He was looking where Rowe had been, not where he now was.

In a gentling tone Rowe said, 'When we get back I'll stand you to all the hay you can eat an' a hat full of rolled barley. How'd you like that?'

The answer came from the nearest stand of trees. 'You ain't goin' back. *Don't move!* Don't even breathe. Empty that holster, you son of a bitch!'

Rowe hadn't moved. He only moved his right arm now to tug loose the tie-down thong over his holstered Colt.

'All the way, you bastard. Lift it out'n let it drop!'

Rowe let the six-gun fall. His left hand still rested on the horse's neck. How someone had left the cabin and soundlessly followed him around to the horse . . . with moccasined feet?

'If you got a belly-gun . . . '

'I got no belly-gun,' Rowe interrupted to say and started to turn. The pistol barrel was jammed into his back with force.

'I said don't move!'

Rowe flinched.

The fiercely angry voice was raised. 'I got the bastard. Come see who he is!'

Rowe straightened up slowly. The

122

gun barrel over the kidneys would have put most men on the ground. He and his captor stared.

The hand holding the six-gun noticeably sagged. 'For Chris'sake!'

Another man materialized from the darkness as Rowe said, 'Josh, what in hell . . . '

Burke Arnold came close, stopped and stared before turning to Rowe's captor. For a long moment nothing was said, not until the marshal spoke. 'Josh, I'm goin' to break your gawddamned neck.'

Davidson showed shock in every line in his face. 'You!' He faced his employer. 'I don't believe this, Burke.'

The cowman did not take his eyes off Rowe when he replied to his top hand. 'He's got her tied up in there. Go set her loose, Josh.'

Rowe spoke quickly. 'Don't go near that cabin, Josh. I think there's two of 'em in there. One is that feller named Humes who's been hangin' around town. He's got Alice.'

Burke Arnold looked around for something to sit on. There was nothing so he straightened up facing the marshal.

'What the hell are you talkin' about? We tracked Elise's horse up here. Who's in there?'

The back pain was severe otherwise Rowe might have answered differently.

'I just told you who he is. He took Alice with him from the café. He's got her in there sure as I'm standin' here. It's not your daughter, you old bastard, it's Alice Gordon. I trailed him up here. She's ridin' double with him, and he's leadin' a horse . . . Elise?'

The range boss turned with an upraised arm. 'You see that stocking-footed chestnut out with them other two horses? That's Elise's special animal. She went huntin' some cut backs we figured come up in here somewhere.' Davidson let his arm drop as he scowled at Rowe. 'Someone's got 'em both in there? That woman who's got the café an' Elise Arnold?'

Rowe glared from Davidson to the older man he worked for.

'Maybe I should've recognized that stocking-footed horse. Burke, what's the matter with you, lettin' Elise go prowl around up in here?'

Arnold reset his hat as he answered. 'Who is he? Humes? I don't recollect anyone by that name. He's got both of 'em in there? Is he crazy? I'm goin' to smoke that son of a bitch out of there if it's the last thing I ever do. Josh?'

The range boss was re-tying the tie-down over his holstered Colt when Rowe hit him. Davidson wobbled ten feet backwards before falling. A spit-back of blood appeared at the corner of his mouth.

Burke Arnold dropped his right shoulder with fingers coiled toward the pistol butt. Rowe caught him by the coat up high, lifted him off his feet and shook him like a coyote shaking a squirrel. Then pushed him away.

Josh rolled over and groaned. He dug in the ground until he could get onto all fours. He hung there looking dazedly from side to side.

Rowe leaned, got one fistful of riding coat and reared back with a grunt.

He had to hold the range boss upright or he would have collapsed.

Rowe let go. The range boss fell against Burke Arnold as Rowe released his grip on the older man. Arnold didn't fall but he almost did.

The grulla horse hadn't moved. Rowe leaned on him. The pain was less severe, but it clearly wasn't going to stop soon.

As Burke Arnold steadied his range boss he asked why Rowe had struck Davidson. He didn't get an answer.

In fact, until the older man asked Rowe for a full explanation the marshal didn't speak. When he told Burke Arnold what he knew and what he now suspected the cowman seemed incapable of putting all of it together to create an understandable situation. His range boss had a purplish swelling on one side of his lower face. It made his words sound differently than they normally sounded. While he talked he avoided looking directly at the marshal.

When Rowe wanted to know where the other B A riders were their employer said he had left them with the gather north of town, that he and the range boss had been so upset at not finding the old man's daughter that they hadn't deviated from their hunt.

Burke Arnold wanted to know everything he could about the man who had evidently abducted his daughter.

To Rowe it seemed clear that somewhere between the holding area north of town and the log house, Humes and his hostage from the café had encountered Elise Arnold. The rest of the conclusion was simple enough: Humes had probably used a gunpoint to herd the old man's daughter toward the log house in its stump-country clearing.

Rowe told the older man everything he knew about the abductor, most of it was a repetition of what Bryan

Cullom had told him.

Burke Arnold was agitated. So was his range boss who hadn't said much since his recovery from being struck by the one man in Fleming township of whom it was said that when he hit someone with either of his iron-handed fists they not only avoided Rowe Harmon, with the identical avoidance most folks reserved for rattlers, or mothering cougars, they didn't go anywhere in town he might be.

It was Josh Davidson who commented on the imminence of dawn. His employer passed through timber toward the north side of the log house and was standing there when the light inside lost about half of its brilliance.

He returned where the marshal and his range boss were making clumsy attempts at amelioration to tell them he was going to offer the unseen abductor $1,000 for the release of his hostages.

Neither of the men he told this to seemed agreeable. Rowe wanted Humes's hide. The range boss reminded his employer that he didn't carry a sixty-foot lariat for the exclusive use of roping break-away cattle. Sixty feet was about right for a hang rope.

The older man went back to his earlier position to call out his offer and to await an answer which came eventually: Humes would release both women on two considerations; that the ransom would be increased to $5,000 and that Burke Arnold would pass his word that he would lead the way back down to Fleming for everyone who was out there with him.

The older man did not return to tell his range boss and the marshal about the counter offer, he simply agreed and said he would have to go back to his ranch for the money.

Humes wanted to know how long that would take and when Arnold replied, 'Until tomorrow afternoon to get there, and the same amount of time to get back,' Humes answered sourly, 'An' a few extra hours to round up a posse. Go back, old man, do some ponderin' an' come back when you got somethin' better to offer. An' don't fret, we got plenty of black-eyed peas an' whatnot to keep us goin' for quite a spell . . . Mr Arnold?'

'Yes?'

'She's downright pretty as a picture, this daughter of yours.'

Burke Arnold returned. Rowe and the range boss listened to the older man and unanimously and almost simultaneously said they would never agree to anything that meant the women would stay overnight with Chris Humes in light of what they had heard about him and his obsession.

7

A Mexican Stand-off

They were squatting like Indians when dawn light brightened the clearing. Burke Arnold saw no alternative to buying the hostages, which he was willing to do. He suggested that his range boss and Fleming's marshal stay in place, keep the forted-up abductor occupied while Arnold went back for the money and returned.

Davidson was undecided and talked very little. His jaw was swollen and painful. It was the marshal who opposed giving Humes anything. His back was as painful as a boil.

Burke Arnold arose as he said, 'There's no other way. That bastard is forted up in there with a sighting in every direction.'

He was ready to go back where his

horse was tethered and leave the high country.

Rowe looked steadily at the older man. 'You can't make the ride an' return until late tomorrow. I'm not goin' to leave Alice with Humes that long. Not after what I know about him.'

Josh Davidson was gingerly exploring his jaw when he shook his head at his employer. 'You go ahead; do what you got to do. I'll stay here with Rowe. We might get lucky. If we do when you get back you'll see that son of a bitch hangin' from a tree.'

Arnold hesitated. 'Don't you boys do anythin' that'll upset that crazy bastard. Keep him talkin' until I get back. You understand me? That's my daughter in there.'

Nothing was said until Burke Arnold was leaving, then Rowe called out, 'Bring back food'n a bottle of fire water.'

Arnold kept on walking. Rowe and the range boss smoked. Davidson had trouble but he persevered. He even attempted to smile when the marshal said, 'You look like hell.'

The range boss had an answer but it was difficult to understand so he laboriously repeated it.

'I heard around town you'n Alice was fixin' to get married. If she could see you right now . . . '

Rowe interrupted. 'Josh, when you're back to normal I'm gonna stand you up an' whip the whey out of you.'

The range boss would have argued, but because the swelling was increasing, not diminishing, and he knew he was difficult to understand he offered no reply beyond gingerly probing the place where he'd been hit, and shaking his head.

Rowe wanted to go to his horse and off-saddle. There were two flat tins of sardines in the saddlebags, a range-man's alternative to starving. When he leaned to ratchet himself upright the pain in his back spread. He gave it up.

Someone called from the log house. 'Hey, cowman, how much cash money you got with you?'

Rowe and the range boss looked at each other. Rowe dug deep and came up with seven crumpled greenbacks and a sprinkling of coins.

Josh emptied his pockets of money, three greenbacks and close to another dollar in coins. He said, 'I can't yell. Call back that we got three thousand dollars.'

Rowe's eyes briefly widened before he said, 'He'll know we're lyin' an' take it out on the women.'

Josh fought to make his words understandable. 'He's goin' to kill 'em anyway.'

Rowe turned to the right. The pain was like a red-hot poker. He settled back as Davidson said, 'Try it to the left.'

Rowe moved slowly and carefully. He stopped moving, looked at his companion, settled back for a moment then tried again, this time with less caution.

The range boss made a lopsided grin.

'I jammed you on the right side. Try standin' up.'

As Josh said this he rocked far back and forward, jockeyed himself into a standing position and extended a hand.

Rowe gripped the extended fingers, very gingerly took a step, winced slightly and took another step.

Only when he would have turned right in the direction of his horse did the pain appear. Still holding the other man's hand he turned left. The pain was very slight. He released his grip on the extended hand, turned further left, walked about half a yard, turned to the left and walked back. Josh was forcing a grin. It cost him to do it, but he held the expression until Rowe got back into a sitting position on the ground, then he also sat down.

Rowe arose hesitantly again, made a half circle to the left, reached his horse and foraged in a saddle-bag until he found the flat tins, then turned left again and eased down opposite the range boss.

As Rowe put one of the little flat tins into Davidson's lap he said, 'Right after you jammed me I could hardly draw a breath.'

As Josh fumbled with the small container he said, 'When I was a button my pa got mule kicked where I rammed you with the pistol. You're luckier'n he was. He couldn't even stand up for two days, an' after that he could only turn one way. My ma cooked his back red as a beet with hot wraps.'

'How long before he could turn both ways?'

'If I recollect right it was about a week.'

Nothing more was said between them until they had eaten all the little fish and had drained the oil, after which the range boss said, 'I never liked them things nor the oil but for a fact they kill a man's hunger and put him off gettin' real thirsty . . . Rowe?'

Rowe finished piling stones on his empty tin as he replied, 'What?'

'You stay here. I'm goin' to run those

horses out of the clearing.'

Rowe had to turn completely before he could see the grazing animals. The range boss was already on his feet. 'Set the bastard afoot,' he said to Rowe. 'I got a bad feelin' about this bird. Burke won't get back until tomorrow. If that bastard . . . what's his name?'

'Humes. Chris Humes.'

'If he's *coyote* he'll sneak out before dawn, get a horse an' come mornin' he'll be fifteen miles on his way.'

Rowe considered the range boss. He knew from local talk that Davidson was a top hand. Top hands were stockmen. He grinned. 'Go do it,' he said, 'but if he opens the door he'll see you.'

Davidson returned the smile. 'He won't see me.'

Rowe watched the older man work his way northward in among the trees. The grazing horses were about halfway toward the northernmost part of the clearing. Rowe wasn't convinced the stockman could bring it off. If he failed and spooked the horses Humes might be able to hear them running.

Moving was uncomfortable but not cripplingly so. Rowe got to his feet and did as the range boss had done, but in the opposite direction. Carrying the Winchester didn't make the pain less, even when he shifted it to his left hand. He thought of leaning it aside. About the time he decided to do so a wolf sounded from southward down about where the trail left the clearing.

Rowe paused. The wolf did not sound again nor did Rowe catch a glimpse of it.

He got into a position where he could see the log wall's northerly side. If Humes came out in front Rowe wouldn't be able to see him unless he moved clear of the door in the direction of the horses.

He could see the split and the stump where he'd been earlier and wished he could get over there now. From the split he would have a perfect view of the entire front of the house and the doorway.

It was too late to try and get over there. Josh would by now be far enough northward to move eastward toward the three horses.

He inched closer until he could see the three horses and stopped stone still. They were standing like statues peering intently toward the area where the range boss would be. What he saw was the brush where a half-grown wolf was running with his tail straight out behind.

He was satisfied; Josh was down there. The horses could have been spooked by the wolf.

He returned his attention to the log house. It occurred to him that it was awfully quiet over there. Humes and his hostages had been holed up in there an awfully long time. Someone had to come out, sometime.

His attention was caught by the sound of running horses. He had a fleeting glimpse before they disappeared amid the trees.

He waited for Humes to open the

door. Nothing like that happened. The sound may not have penetrated the log walls.

He went back where he and the range boss had been. When Josh arrived he said, 'It wasn't me. There was a bitch wolf down there with three pups. She saw me and cut between me'n her pups. That spooked the horses.' As the range boss sat down he also said, 'Are you a bettin' man?'

Rowe shrugged. 'What on?'

'That Burke'll come onto those horses. Elise's horse knows where home is.'

Rowe smiled. 'No bet.'

He had barely spoken when there was a noise from the cabin and both watchers stood up, Rowe with his Winchester in his left hand.

Nothing happened. Humes did not appear nor did either of the women. Josh sighed and dropped back down. 'Take turns; you keep watch while I nap.'

Rowe went forward as far as the

140

thinning trees and considered the house. Humes was acting like he knew his enemies were close. Rowe lowered his head. The sun was beginning to poke its rays between tree branches. As he was turning back he heard steel scrape over stone, knelt and watched until he saw a rider coming up that stingy trail from the south. The man was sitting straight up. He had seen the cabin and was studying it.

As nearly as Rowe could see the man was nobody he had seen before, even though everything about him seemed familiar, the way he sat the saddle, the way he was dressed, even the shapeless old hat he wore. Whoever he was there was no doubt but that he was a rangeman.

Rowe went back and awakened Josh. They returned together to the place where Rowe had been. Josh made a long, squinty-eyed study and shook his head. 'No one I know. You expect Humes'n his partners get visitors up here?' Before Rowe could answer the range boss answered his own question. 'I don't think so, unless maybe it's a friend of theirs.'

They watched the rider halt where the cleared ground ended. He was partly in shadow. Rowe had the impression the rider had never been up here before. He said, 'If he knocks on that door . . . '

Josh nodded and grunted as the horseman started for the front of the log house. He swung off trailing one rein and hit the door twice with his fist. The response he got was not one he expected.

Humes called out in a growly loud voice, 'Mister Cowman you're goin' to get yourself shot. You got the money?'

The horseman took a step back before speaking. 'My name's Will Hampton. I met a feller down yonder a ways. He told me he was a friend from town of the man who owns a ranch down here there-abouts. He said wasn't no one around. I asked him where the nearest town was an' he give me directions. I come onto a trail an' followed it. How far to that town he mentioned?'

There was a long delay before the answer came back. 'That's the sorriest lie I ever heard. I'm goin' to shoot through the door.'

The stranger jumped sideways so quickly he almost tripped. He didn't toe into the stirrup, he vaulted and hooked his horse hard. The animal jumped ahead and lit down running. Rowe and Josh had a very brief glimpse of the man's face. Neither one of them recognized him.

They watched him until he reined up before entering the forest. The range boss turned back toward the cabin just in time to hear the door being slammed closed. He said, 'Why would someone tell him to use the trail leading up here?'

Rowe didn't answer because he couldn't.

Davidson surprised the marshal when he pulled a watch from a pocket, flipped the case open and closed it. Rowe had no idea Burke Arnold's head Indian even owned a watch let alone carried one.

Josh said, 'Gettin' nigh onto ten o'clock.' He made a rueful grin. 'You're a lawman, can't you come up with somethin'? I'm hungry an' thirsty. We're goin' to be up here all day and maybe another damned long night.'

Rowe didn't mention his own hunger and thirst except to say he wondered where the men who had made the log house had got their water. 'Got to be a spring somewhere around,' he stated, and went back to the topic of the stranger.

It didn't take long to exhaust that topic. Josh went looking for a creek or a spring. Rowe went to look after his horse; he let it browse until the range boss returned with a dented, rusty coffee tin. It was two thirds full of spring water. Rowe drank it down while his companion was explaining where he'd found the spring.

Except for the stranger they had pretty well run out of things to talk about and their conclusion about him was that he was one of those drifters who worked when they found it and who otherwise drifted; kept riding. Every working season they appeared and just as often they didn't work, they drifted. That decision depended on how much money they still had from their last place of employment.

The sun was behind where they were sitting, waiting. Evidently boredom was a two-way road. Humes called from the cabin, 'Anyone out there? I got a trade for you. One of the women for you to look north so's I can ride south.'

Rowe made a sardonic grin as he called back. 'That'd be a tolerable swap except that you don't have anythin' to ride away on.'

Humes did not respond for several minutes during which Josh made an observation that hit close to home. 'Marshal, the son of a bitch hasn't opened the door. He don't know the horses're gone.'

Rowe raised his voice. 'Humes, you're not goin' anywhere. Look outside. There aren't no horses.'

This time the reply was even more delayed. During it Josh said, 'The son of a bitch! We should've been over yonder where that split is. We could've nailed him when he poked his head out.'

Rowe shrugged. They had missed an opportunity but he had an idea. 'We can make his trade, Josh. Tell him that.'

The range boss did. 'Holmes, or whatever your name is, turn the woman loose an' you start walkin'. We'll give you as much time as you'll need to get among them trees that line both sides of that southward trail.'

Humes's retort was edged with impatience. 'It's Humes, not Holmes. As for the rest of it . . . I wouldn't trust you as far as I could throw you. Unless you want to move out where I can see you . . . take you with me. You leave your guns behind.'

Josh made a little fluttery gesture with both hands and lowered his voice so that it wouldn't carry. 'Take a chance. Tell him to put the woman outside an' I'll walk over there. If he thinks there's only one of us . . . '

Rowe interrupted. 'He knows there's two of us. At least two. We both been talkin' to him.' Rowe raised his voice. 'All right; I'll start walkin' when I see the woman.'

Humes's answer settled the question. He called back, 'Which one of you?'

Rowe pulled a dour smile and his companion did the same. He raised his voice when he said, 'Which one you want?'

'The marshal. I'll turn loose the woman he wants to marry.' Humes laughed. 'Undamaged goods. Her name's Alice.' Humes's voice went a little louder. 'Marshal, ain't that a good swap?'

Josh answered before Rowe had the opportunity. 'You'll lose out on the money Mr Arnold's fetchin' back.'

'I'll risk it. Which one are you?'

'Josh Davidson, the old man's range boss. Are we goin' to talk a leg off or make a trade?'

Humes did not respond. Rowe fidgeted. His companion shook his head. 'You know what he's doin'? Figurin'. Settin' in there figurin' how he can get the money an' make a run for it.'

Rowe balanced the saddle gun across his lap, eyed the house and softly cursed. If there had been a window in that north wall . . .

Humes broke the silence. 'It'll be dark directly.'

Josh had an answer for that. 'That'll be in your favour.'

The silence settled again and Josh Davidson used the time to lift out his six-gun, examine it, spin the cylinder and ease it back into its holster.

Humes called, 'The both of you walk out where I can see you. I'll be behind the woman . . . all right?'

Josh made another observation. 'He's gettin' desperate.' He called back, 'Just one of us comes out.'

This time the forted-up man's answer was tinged with sarcasm. 'Range boss, I didn't come down in the last rain. Your partner shoots from cover. More'n likely he'll hit the woman but just as likely he'll hit me.'

Rowe couldn't resist. He said, 'No loss, you son of a bitch.'

Humes took that personally. 'You better mind your mouth, mister, or I'll push her out an' shoot her where you can see her fall.'

Josh Davidson softly said, 'I'm goin' to gut shoot that bastard,' and Rowe replied in the same lowered voice, 'You'll have to get in line.' He paused, leaned as far as he dared and looked upwards. 'Burke's had enough time.' He returned his attention to the range boss. 'Keep him talkin'. I'm goin' far enough south to get behind the house then try to slip in close on the far side.'

Josh said nothing as he watched the

marshal arise, hoist the carbine with his left hand and move soundlessly southerly. Shortly before Rowe passed from sight he called after him, 'You'll need the luck of the Irish.'

The answer he got back was trite. 'Maybe I can borrow a little.'

After Rowe had been gone Humes called again. 'Who was that horsebacker who came up out front?'

Josh replied indifferently. 'Saddle tramp. I never saw him before. Neither did the marshal.'

'He come within an ace of gettin' himself killed. You're sure he wasn't some friend of one or t'other of you, or maybe one of the old man's riders?'

'I'm sure. I worked somethin' like ten years for the old man, I never saw him before in my life.'

After another lull Humes said, 'I'll give you the spitfire. If someone ever marries her he'll live to regret it. She's got the makings of a bitch wolf.'

'All right. Turn her out.'

This time the lull was longer. Josh

used it to get recklessly closer to the final skimpy trace of trees, mostly thinned out by the cabin builders.

The sun was so far down in the west it couldn't even make a decent showing. Southward, cabin logs had been downed and skived for quite a few yards behind the house. Josh could see in that direction and there was no sign of the marshal.

Rowe was down there behind the westerly wall. He eased ahead with infinite care. He did not have to worry about Humes picking up sounds; the pine and fir needles were ankle deep, layered upon one another to a depth of possibly five to six inches.

A bird as large as a big chicken soared in out of nowhere, made a clumsy landing, juggled its footing, either saw or scented the wingless thing below and with a squawk sprang into the air and went in flawless flight deeper into the forest.

Rowe watched the bird out of sight and resumed his foot-at-a-time forward stalk until he was close to the rear wall.

Where he halted there was an array of knee-high stumps, mostly old enough to show lumps of hardened resin. He selected the tallest stump and hunkered down behind it. He could see adequately in three directions, north and south where anyone coming to the meadow from those directions would be visible in carbine range.

Looking easterly he was close enough to the log wall to count knots.

Somehow that lowering sun worked its way through the timber and was reflected in his eyes.

There was neither movement nor sound.

8

Horsebacking

Someone inside the cabin was cooking. Smoke coming from the stove pipe in puffs carried a tantalizing aroma. Rowe inhaled deeply and exhaled. He leaned against a tree. At the moment he was willing to run a reckless risk and he might have done it if someone speaking quietly hadn't provided a startling diversion.

The range boss said, 'I'm goin' to rap on the back wall.'

Rowe went to work manufacturing a cigarette. 'What'll that do?'

Davidson replied irritably. 'Stir him up, maybe.'

Rowe offered the makings which Davidson declined by shaking his head.

Rowe squinted upwards. 'Burke'll be along directly. We've gone this long,

153

another hour or so hadn't ought to matter. What's someone cookin' in there?'

'Smells like spuds'n maybe meat.'

The range boss fished in a pocket, brought forth a plug, worried off a thick sliver and pouched it. He expectorated once before saying, 'That house is mighty dry.'

Rowe's forehead formed several furrows. 'Not while I'm here,' he said. 'Besides, you set it afire, bein' the time of year it is the fire'll burn for miles.'

'Wait for Burke?'

'Like I said, Josh, we waited this long. He's got to show up directly. Let's go back. That smell's got my gut thinkin' my throat's been cut.'

They were halfway back when a noise from the cabin stopped them dead still. It was followed by a door being swung so violently it collided with a wall.

Rowe turned. As they started back he said, 'If he's out — shoot!'

Burke Arnold's dishevelled daughter appeared. She faced half around as the

154

range boss called, 'Elise!'

The lithe woman paused only for a moment then ran back inside. The men outside were close enough to hear her loudly say, 'Hold still!'

Rowe, followed by Josh Davidson came inside and stopped stone still. Elise Arnold blocked their view of the woman tied to one of the homemade beds. Elise was working with a wicked-bladed fleshing knife.

Rowe moved fast. Using his own clasp knife he cut hard-twist manila lariat rope. Between the two of them they got Alice into a sitting position. She was shaking and where her clothing had been ripped and torn there were dark bruises.

Josh stepped over the man on the floor. He picked up several pieces of the lariat rope, knelt and tied Humes's ankles. He would have done the same higher up at the unconscious man's arms but a groan stopped him. Between them they got Humes to a stool, dragged a table close to prop his back and the range boss looked for something to wipe his hands on. Rowe took Alice outside where dusk was settling, kept her walking over as far as the split tree and back until she fell against him being shaken by deep-down sobs.

Josh came out holding a cooking utensil. It was a cast-iron fry pan with a hook in the wooden handle for suspending it. Josh helped get Alice to a rough log bench near the barn and held up the skillet as he said, 'This is what she hit him with. I think the son of a bitch is dead.'

Rowe left the range boss with Alice. Inside, Elise Arnold met him looking impassively haggard and rumpled. She went to a wall bunk and sank down. 'They came up out of a draw,' she said in a dull voice. 'They were riding double. I thought . . . I don't know what I thought. He pointed his Colt at me and cocked it.' She stopped looking up at the marshal. 'He brought us here. Rowe . . . ?'

'Leave it be, Elise. Your pa'll be

along. He left to get the ransom money.'

She didn't seem to be listening. Her gaze dropped back to the floor. 'All the way up here he kept telling us what he was going to do. Once Alice fainted and fell off. He used his six-gun to make me help get her back behind him in the saddle. She is tough and strong, Marshal. She tried to fight him. That's how she got hurt'n all. He tied her to the bed. He tied me by the ankles to a saddle rack. He made us eat, all the time describing how he would do . . . things . . . He was crazy, Rowe. Plumb crazy. He told us how he'd done . . . things before . . . like he was going to do to us. See that bottle by the fireplace? He made us drink. He drank most of it. Then he really talked — and laughed. Told us how he'd handled folks who resisted.' She paused to raise her eyes again. 'Is he dead?'

Rowe did not know and did not leave the woman to find out. She spoke again, this time with more feeling in what she said.

'It wasn't just the women he'd caught out. He robbed three banks and killed a storekeeper for not having as much money as he thought the storekeeper should've had.

'He killed a little boy for not knowing where his parents kept their savings-money . . . Rowe?'

' 'Lise, settle back. I'll get Josh to set with you.'

'No! Take me outside.'

'It's cold, 'Lise.'

She stood up. 'The air'll be cleaner.' She held out a hand. He led her from the cabin to where Josh made room for her beside Alice. Until now she had managed, but the moment she and Alice were together they fell into each other's arms and cried.

Rowe looked at Josh Davidson who returned the look and nodded his head. He would stay with the women.

Rowe returned to the cabin. The smell was sickening. He got Humes to one of the wall bunks. He was bloody from the head to the waist and although he was able to help getting to the bunk, Rowe was ready to believe he wouldn't last much longer. Rowe examined the cabin, the crudely made cupboards, the bunks, even two back bundles which had been ransacked, their contents scattered.

He found a whiskey bottle, half full, and from which the label had been torn off.

When Humes fought to sit up Rowe helped, got him propped against the log wall and got some whiskey down him.

He had been struck from behind. By visual reconstruction Rowe pieced together what had happened. He had no idea *how* it had happened, but when Humes had been feeding the stove he had been hit from behind by that solid cast-iron fry pan.

It should have killed him. Those big old skillets were heavy; Rowe remembered seeing some very strong men lift them and some strong women use both hands to lift them.

How Elise Arnold had got behind him would require considerable explaining. How she had managed to lift the skillet high enough to bring it down on his head would require even more explaining because, while Elise was known for her strength, how she had managed this time would be even harder to explain.

While Rowe was examining an old Army issue Sharps carbine, the man on the bunk loudly groaned and fought to stand up.

He might not have made it if another strong man hadn't been close.

Rowe pushed Humes back down, told him to stay there and went after the whiskey bottle.

Humes drank deeply, handed back the bottle and passed out.

Rowe was arranging him on the bedding when Josh Davidson came inside. At the scowl he got from the marshal he said, 'The women'll be fine.'

He came closer to gaze at the man on the cot and say, 'I'll find some water. He's got to be conscious when he's hung.'

They threw whatever had been cooking on the stove outside and each got down two swallows from Humes's bottle.

The range boss smiled. About two-thirds of his facial swelling was gone. He looked critically at the marshal. 'You're gettin' around better.'

Until he'd been told that the marshal hadn't even thought of his injury. They each had one more swallow before leaving the cabin.

Outside Rowe got another surprise. Elise's father was holding his daughter over on the corral bench.

He approached Alice who looked up at him with her unchanged dull expression. She started to cry and he held her.

The horses needed care. Josh went to do what could be done. There was hay in the loft but an animal would have to be very hungry to eat it. The hay was dry with mouse tunnels and spider webs.

As fast as Josh pitched it down the horses ate it. For a long moment the range boss leaned on the fork standing motionless in the loft opening. His hunger had been appeased by what his employer had brought back with him. He had also brought a bottle from his private stock. It was brandy. Josh Davidson was a lifelong rangeman; they only drank whiskey.

The B A rider who had come with Elise's father had red hair and a crooked nose, caused by running face-first into someone's fist. His name was Cardiff. Moses Cardiff. He was called Red.

When the range boss left the barn he asked Red if he and Burke had found three loose horses.

They had. According to Cardiff one animal belonged to Elise. Red was of the opinion that if those horses hadn't followed them back, Elise's gelding would have taken the other two home to the ranch.

Alice's recovery was slower than Elise Arnold's recovery.

Elise would have gone to the cabin with her father if he hadn't expressly forbidden it.

The older man did not say a word when he and Chris Humes gazed at each other.

In fact, Humes didn't speak as the others went about doing whatever chores required doing. He only spoke with feeling when Burke Arnold said that after the house had been cleared of everything, he would set it afire.

Humes fiercely opposed that idea. Rowe thought that as one of those who had built the cabin, which had required strenuous effort, Humes had reason to object.

Red came to tell the range boss the three horses that followed them back needed feeding. Josh took the rider with him to help pitch out more feed.

Elise came to the doorway. She and

Humes exchanged a long stare before she returned to the yard with her father. Beginning with when she had been caught by Humes she told him everything that had happened including the reason why Humes had tied Alice Gordon to the bed — he listened without interruption.

Rowe and the range boss went several times to the place where Burke Arnold had left a pair of saddlebags. By the time their hunger had been appeased there was little left. Rowe thought they had ought to rig out and aim for the low country.

While he and Josh Davidson were preparing the animals to be loaded, Burke Arnold came over and said he would send Red and his range boss on ahead to start the cattle drive through Fleming.

The range boss and the hired rider nodded, but Rowe faced the older man and said, 'Leave it be, Burke. I would've thought you'd started the drive yestiddy.'

Arnold scowled. 'Elise was gone. By the time Josh and I found the tracks where she'd rode toward the highlands it was too late, an' she was more important than all the cattle drives I ever made.'

'You left one rider with the drive?' Rowe asked and the older man shook his head. 'There was both the riders with 'em. They wouldn't do anythin' until Josh'n me got back. Since I brought Red back here with me, that leaves only one man with the gather, not enough if they scatter. He'll just try to hold 'em until I find him. You ready with those horses, Marshal?'

Rowe nodded and drifted his attention in the direction of the log house. 'What about *him*?'

Josh answered. 'We got time to hang him.'

Red was near the house when he called to the others. 'Better hurry up if you figure to hang him. He's about bled out.'

Elise took her father aside. When they

returned where the others were standing Elise's father said, 'Get astride. Let's head down out of here.'

For a moment not a word was said. Not until the old cowman's girl spoke aside to the range boss and he took time to reset his hat and to tell Red to get astride and lead the way back to lower country using the same trail that they had used getting up here.

Red and Rowe exchanged a look before the rider got astride and led off. When Josh had a chance he got up beside the marshal. When Rowe nodded and said, 'Dead, back there.' The range boss gazed steadily at Rowe without speaking. Moments later they were trailing out of the clear and into the timber. From that point on there was little opportunity for any of them to ride stirrup to stirrup.

The way back had to be covered cautiously. Being in timber was bad enough but in almost complete darkness other obstacles such as boulders and deadfall logs made it necessary for the riders to watch every step.

The range boss was riding directly behind his employer. Now and then they would lean to speak but the colder it became the less often they did that.

Elise's horse stumbled to both knees. She left the saddle and led the way. The horse had no difficulty after he was being led instead of ridden.

By the time they reached Custer Creek and stopped to water the animals the red-maned B A rider sidled up to the marshal to say he'd wager his saddle it was close to freezing.

Rowe nodded; he believed the hired rider was right. He had another reason for bypassing this opportunity to talk. He left the grulla at the creek to approach Elise Arnold with a question. 'Was he dead back there?'

If Elise had inherited anything from her father it was a tendency toward brusqueness. She replied to the marshal curtly. 'You can go back and see for yourself.'

Rowe pondered that answer, shrugged

and turned to walk back where the grulla was dripping water. She stopped him.

'If he wasn't dead when we left up there he will be tomorrow, when my father sends one of the riders up there to set the cabin on fire.'

Alice was shivering beside her horse, which was the animal Chris Humes had used as a pack animal. Rowe shook out of his jacket for her. When she protested he smiled, kissed her cheek and covered the short distance to the grulla and swung astride. When the redheaded B A rider would have resumed the trail in the direction of Burke Arnold's home place, the old man told his range boss to aim for Fleming.

In flat country it was possible for riders to travel in pairs. The range boss came up beside Rowe, offered his plug and when the offer was refused the range boss said, 'When we reach town I'm goin' to hire a room an' sleep for a week.'

Rowe was scratching his growth of

whiskers when he replied. 'He'll fire you. He's headin' for town so's he can drive those damned cattle through like he's done for years. He'll need you'n every rider he can get. Half the folks in town are against him doin' that.'

The range boss surprised Rowe with his answer. 'Fire me if he likes. Somethin' like eight years back when I hired on with him I was lookin' for work . . . I'll be doin' the same when he fires me. Rowe? He hadn't ought to do that. Except that he's got a notion it shows folks he can drive where he wants to; he's got no right to dirty the road for the full length of Fleming, an' upset folks.'

Rowe gazed at the man beside him. 'Did you ever tell him that?'

'No, but it's been bothering me for years. I'll tell him. When we get to town I'll tell him'n go into town to hire a room.'

Burke sent Red Cardiff on ahead to tell the rider down at Fleming he was coming; for the pair of them to bunch the cattle to be ready.

Elise eased back to ride with Rowe. She was a very attractive woman in a slightly domineering way. Being single and the daughter of the best set-up cowman further than folks could see gave her the right to be as she was.

As she and the marshal rode together she said, 'You could go ahead an' make sure that Biblebanger's flock don't try to make trouble for the drive.'

Rowe faced the handsome woman. 'I could, for a fact, but those protesters bein' mostly women maybe if you went ahead they'd listen to you rather'n me.'

They rode together in silence until Arnold's daughter loped ahead to ride with her father.

Once Burke twisted in the saddle to look in the marshal's direction, but that interlude only lasted moments.

They made better time in flat country despite the fact that they were straddling tired horses.

By the time they had distant rooftops

in sight, particularly the tall, white-painted church steeple, the day had worn well along.

Burke turned back to ride with the marshal. He avoided the customary preliminaries when he said, 'It's your job, Rowe. That idea of Elise goin' ahead to keep folks calm wouldn't work. She bein' my daughter would more'n likely make things worse.'

Rowe smiled at the older man. 'I figured woman to women might work. I'm the law; they wouldn't like me throwin' down on 'em. They'd figure it different if Elise talked . . . calmed 'em down.'

Josh Davidson came over and reined in on the marshal's opposite side. He leaned to speak to Burke and ignored Rowe.

'Burke, why not let the drive wait a day or two. Some of us been without eatin' or sleepin' for a long time.'

Rowe waited for what else the range boss might say. Burke Arnold left no time for a retort.

'Josh, we been doin' this since a year or two before you got hired on. This same month an' this same day.'

Rowe sensed what was coming and spoke next. 'Burke, I'm bone tired. Josh's got to be too. An' you, ridin' down here'n back. Even if the horses wasn't rode down, we deserve a rest. Aren't none of us made of iron.'

Elise left off riding with Alice and reined in on the far side of her father. She had to lean around him to address the marshal.

'We talked, Rowe. I'm tired. So is Alice. So are you. It's nearest for us to rest at the ranch and get fed than it would be if we rode to town.'

Rowe saw the range boss watching him and said, 'That's not it, Elise. I'll give up a few more hours of sleep an' a decent female-cooked meal.'

'Then what is it, Rowe?'

'You know as well as I do.' He also had to lean around her father. 'When I left town folks was squaring off about the cattle.'

She hovered briefly as though to argue then settled back in the saddle. 'All right. We'll go to town, but it'll be settled by now.'

Her father, silent until now, said, 'What in hell is there to get folks so upset? I been drivin' through town . . . it's sort of a celebration, has been for years. The children get a kick out of it. So does Hersheimer. He picks up a little money he otherwise wouldn't get.'

Rowe refused to relent. 'I got a prisoner in the jailhouse. He'll be hungry by now.'

Burke and his daughter said no more. They continued to ride with the marshal until his daughter turned aside to ride with Alice.

9

One More Day

Red Cardiff broke over into a lope which annoyed Rowe and the range boss. The horses had earned the kind of thoughtful consideration that tired horses earned.

Burke Arnold stood in his stirrups. He was less impatient than he was curious. The distance was too great to make out more than that his cattle were scattered on both sides of the road beyond the outskirts of town. He sat back and addressed his daughter without looking at her.

'I don't like to do it, these horses have been rode enough, but we got to gather those damned cattle an' get on with it.'

She neither agreed nor disagreed. Her handsome stocking-legged big

174

chestnut horse was still up in the bit. Whether she knew it or not endurance was bred into thoroughbreds, even some half-thoroughbreds.

Red came loping back with a companion, a tall, lean individual with a drooping moustache. When they were close Red signalled with an upraised arm.

Burke stopped, those with him followed his example.

The stranger was wearing a coat that matched his britches and a conservative beaver-belly tan hat without much of a brim.

He and the B A rider dropped to a walk for the last dozen yards. Josh, riding with Rowe, heard the marshal gasp. He said, 'You know him?'

Rowe answered crisply. 'I know him. He's a deputy US marshal. His name's Woodrow Shultz.'

The range boss did not speak, not even after he and his companions had met the impressive lawman, who introduced himself without offering his hand although he was close enough. Nor did he speak until he had finished his appraisal of the two women and the men. Then he nodded, just barely. At Rowe Harmon he said, 'Good to see you again. Rowe, what you got against that feller in your jailhouse?'

'When we get to town I'll go over that with you, Woody. Right now we been without rest or grub a long time, an' — '

The lean, grey-eyed man interrupted. 'I got patience, Rowe. You know that. These folks likely got it too. Tell me why you got Bryan Cullom locked up an' haven't fed him for a couple of days.'

Burke Arnold was looking straight at the federal marshal when he addressed him. 'Mister, in a minute I'm goin' to ride right over the top of you. My name's Burke Arnold. Nobody holds me up when I got a reason to keep goin'!'

The deputy marshal rested both hands atop his saddle horn and fixed Burke with a steady gaze. 'I know who you are. I been in Fleming since day afore yestiddy. I've heard a lot about you an' your riders. I'm not askin' you to hang an' rattle, I'm tellin' you to!'

Up until this moment none of the men had heeded the women. The marshal had looked longest at them, at their dishevelled appearance. He considered Elise the longest. Neither Marshal Shultz nor the other men were prepared for what happened when Elise flared up at the federal lawman. 'Who do you think you are, giving orders to my father? We're on our way to town, you can ride along or get ridden over!'

The grey-eyed, lean man looked at Elise in silence until he turned his head towards Rowe. 'You want to ride back with me, Rowe? These folks can stay away if they want. I'm not too interested in 'em anyway. Them an' their squabble with the folks in town . . . Rowe?'

Rowe reddened. He did not say a word, he reined the grulla around and started for Fleming.

The federal lawman paused long enough to look triumphantly at Burke and to lift his hat to Elise before he, too, turned back toward the town.

Josh Davidson watched the pair of horsemen go and spoke to his employer. 'That overbearin' son of a bitch . . . Rowe knows him? They sure aren't much alike.'

Burke also watched the riders when he said, 'Let's start the gather.' Again his daughter spoke brusquely. 'You do it. I'm going to take Alice where the two of us can clean up.'

The four men watched the second pair of riders follow in the wake of the first pair.

Josh glared at Red Cardiff and the other B A hired man. 'You two make a big sashay easterly. The boss'n me'll take the west.'

Burke was old enough to keep as much temper as he felt from showing. He rode off with his range boss, neither of them willing to let off steam. Not for a while yet.

What had transpired after the federal marshal and Burke Arnold's crew met, had been watched from doors and windows on both sides of the road that divided Fleming. Mostly, the spying people were discreet. Only a pair of old men out front of the Blue Duck Saloon had the gall to stand in clear sight. They had been warming their cockles inside for some time and buoyed up by Dutch courage made dour remarks until, as the pair of lawmen passed along, Pete Orni caught them both from behind and yanked them back indoors.

Jack Barton was standing in the doorless livery barn opening when the marshal rode up, dismounted and led his grulla horse inside.

The federal officer did the same. Barton called profanely for his hostler to come up front and help.

As the pair of lawmen went up to the jailhouse, Jake Hersheimer came out front of his store and made an announcement in a slightly raised voice.

'Marshal, someone owes me for the

tinned goods I've been supplying your prisoner.'

Rowe raised an arm to indicate he understood and preceded the deputy US marshal inside where he dropped his hat on the table, gestured where the federal man should sit and sank down at his table with an audible sigh. He said, 'Woody, it's been a while.'

As the unsmiling lean man agreed he dug out a matched pair of very dark brown cigars, put one on Rowe's desk and sat on the wall bench to light the other one.

Rowe didn't light the cigar, he put it aside and leaned on the table top. 'Did you talk to my prisoner, Woody?'

The lean man pushed both legs out. 'For an hour. Did you find the one you went after?'

'Found him in a log house up in some pretty rough country.'

'Where is he?'

'Left him for dead up there. That woman who sassed you, she caught him from behind with an iron fry pan.'

'Tell me about her, Rowe. Is she daughter to the old man?'

Rowe nodded. 'His daughter; tougher'n a boiled owl.'

'The old man's big in these parts?'

'I got no idea how many cattle he runs but it's got to be a lot. He keeps four men year' round. You been in town for several days?'

'Little over two days. The place is on pins an' needles about the old man drivin' those cattle out yonder down through town.' The lean man tipped ash and held the cigar long enough to examine its fire, then put it back into his mouth and spoke around it. 'Surprised hell out of me, you bein' the local lawman. Six, seven years back you was herdin' big freight outfits for the Cumberland brothers over in Nebraska.'

Rowe's prisoner dragged a tin cup across the steel bars that formed the front of his cell.

Marshal Shultz waited for the racket to stop then said, 'You got charges that'll nail him? From what he told me . . . '

'He's a rustler. I got the proof. I can hold him until a circuit-ridin' judge gets here.'

The federal lawman crossed his legs at the ankles before speaking. 'I happened to be here because of him. He's wanted down south for robbin' a stage. He picked the wrong one. His stage was carryin' an army payroll. That made it the government's business.'

Rowe leaned back off the table. 'So you want him?'

Shultz nodded his head. 'There's a bounty on him. Six hunnert dollars. Workin' for the government I can't take it. You turn him over to me an' I'll put you in for . . . maybe they'll pay half.'

The US marshal worked the conversation back around where he wanted it. 'What's her name; Liza?'

'Elise. Elise Arnold.' Rowe's gaze perceptibly narrowed. 'She's got a disposition like a bear with a sore behind, but if you're interested . . . '

'I'm interested. I'm about ready to retire.'

'You'n her father didn't hitch horses very well out yonder.'

'I'm not interested in the old man. Does she come to town often?'

Rowe had no idea how to answer that. 'I expect she does when she's got a reason.'

'That other one; she looked like she'd been beat up on.'

'She was. By that son of a bitch we left to die up yonder. She's got a café here in town. We're goin' to get married.'

The US lawman's unwavering grey eyes were fixed on Rowe. 'I got a place at the rooming-house. I'd like to leave your town in the next day or two — with Cullom.'

After the federal lawman departed, Rowe brought his prisoner to the office, handed him the very dark cigar and watched Cullom minutely examine it from the wall bench. Rowe didn't waste time. 'He's got a warrant for you.'

Cullom pocketed the cigar and built a cigarette. After lighting up he said, 'You got another sack of tobacco?'

Rowe shook his head. 'I'll get you one directly. Who looked after you?'

'The storekeeper from across the road. I had to holler myself hoarse. What happened to you?'

'Went after Humes. Caught him in a log house in the high country.'

Cullom trickled smoke. 'Dead?'

'By now he'd ought to be. Did the marshal say how he found you and that there's a bounty on you?'

'He told me. He told me somethin' else: you're a professional mule-skinner.'

Rowe went to the cell-room door and held it open. When he jerked his head Bryan Cullom arose. 'Any way I can buy my way into an escape from here?'

'Get in the cell. I'll fetch you somethin' to eat.'

As Cullom passed down to his cell and watched the door being locked he drily said, 'Don't wait so long with the food this time.'

Rowe crossed to the emporium, counted out money for the storekeeper for feeding his prisoner, and also listened to a tart scolding about not making arrangements for feeding Cullom, then went up as far as Alice's café, read the 'Closed' sign and continued northward to the Blue Duck which only had three customers. The proprietor was reading an ancient newspaper with considerable effort.

Rowe leaned on the bar until the little glass and bottle were in front of him, then answered the barman's question about the arrival of a federal marshal in town. 'I knew him in Nebraska years ago. Why?'

Pete Orni put aside the glasses he had used to read the newspaper and wagged his head. 'He's got a way of not makin' folks like him. Asks questions, don't answer 'em, and don't smile.'

Rowe downed his jolt and stood a moment turning the glass in its sticky little puddle before saying, 'He's hell on wheels with a pistol, Pete.'

'He acts like it. What happened to you?'

Rowe let the question pass without an answer. 'B A'll drive the cattle through tomorrow. Not later than the day after. What's the preacher been up to?'

'Doin' what preachers is good at. Bringin' the Lord into keepin' the cattle out. Even some folks that didn't care are warmin' up to him. Tomorrow? I'll close the saloon an' put wood over the roadway window. Marshal, it's a silly thing to get into a fight over; unless I'm wrong there'll be folks get hurt. There was some cattlemen in the last few days. They side with Burke.' The saloon man scooped up the coins Rowe left on the counter, watched him leave and took out the newspaper, fumbled with the eyeglasses until he was satisfied and went back to laboriously putting words together to make sentences.

This time Rowe went around to the alley doorway of the café and when he knocked Alice opened up, smiled and motioned him inside.

She had not only cleaned up but was wearing a fresh dress. She had been in the process of making a meal. When he inhaled deeply she invited him to stay.

Their conversation was stilted and awkward. This was the first time she had invited him past the counter out front, and she evinced no willingness to discuss what had happened after Humes had entered through her alley-way door and had used a cocked six-gun to make her accompany him to the place where his saddle animal had been hidden.

They talked of other things. She was interested in the federal marshal and Rowe was interested in eating. Alice, with years of experience, was an excellent cook, better in fact under the present circumstances than she was when serving diners at her counter.

Alice Gordon had never been a forward person. As they were finishing the meal she said, 'The moon's close to being full.'

Rowe was finishing his coffee when she made that remark. He looked at her over the rim of the cup. 'Buggy ridin'?'

She smiled. 'If you have nothing else to do.'

He arose, put the napkin aside and also smiled. 'I'll go see if Jack Barton's not goin' to use the rig.'

At the door she said, 'There are other things we can talk about.'

He interpreted that correctly, kissed her on the cheek and walked on air all the way to the livery barn where old Barton had just returned from eating at the only other café in town. He said he'd dust his buggy and put his big, gentle harness mare between the shafts, and watched the marshal hike in the direction of the jailhouse, lustily expectorated and went looking for his hostler, who had gone home. Barton pulled the rig into the runway, got his feather duster and used it vigorously.

At the jailhouse, his prisoner called

that Rowe had missed the federal deputy marshal by no more than ten minutes.

Rowe acknowledged that scrap of information by not replying to it. He also ignored Cullom's second call. His prisoner was hungry.

He did eventually call back that he would bring something to eat directly, and dug out the pig bristle brush he used for making his hat presentable and went to work on the Stetson until the brushing no longer brought forth clouds of dust.

He had time so he also cleaned his boots and went out back to fill a wash basin and shave. That took time. It also made his face sore, but by the time he finished he looked satisfactorily presentable.

His courtship of Alice Gordon had progressed slowly. Her encouragement had by now moved ahead to the point that he felt enough time had passed between them for him to take the bull by the horns.

He almost forgot the small split-hide leather packet old Abe White Tail had given him the previous summer with a guarantee that its contents, when stirred with a smidgin of water would make the café-woman to fall into his arms.

He had to make the mixture by draining the last few drops of rusty water from an old canteen which had been hanging by the rifle rack for several years. He got the sticky mess into a medicine bottle, stoppered it and when he left the jailhouse, locked it from the outside, carrying the little bottle in a shirt pocket.

He hesitated between going directly to the livery barn or over to the Blue Duck.

The saloon won out. The after-lunch trade was beginning to drift in when Pete Orni set up the bottle and shot glass, watched the marshal down a jolt, then wandered northerly along his bar to where a pair of old steadies winked. One old man said, 'I can smell him from here. It'll be the café lady an' he'll bowl her over with that smell.'

His companion passed a softly-spoken judgement. 'Horse liniment.'

Les Welsh, the corralyard boss, came in, settled at the bar, wrinkled his face and glared at the marshal but did not comment. Not until the marshal had departed did Welsh growl, 'What'n hell did he wash in?' When no one answered Welsh gave his own opinion.

'Some of that milk weed crushed'n ground with water. It's a special mix In'ians use. If the bottle ain't stoppered tight that's what it smells like.' One of the old men who had spoken earlier spoke again, this time in a tone tinged with sarcasm.

'How would you know somethin' like that, Mr Welsh? In'ians is the onliest folks know about them things; the bucks douse up with that smell when they're fixin' to go courtin'.'

The corralyard boss downed two jolts, one after the other, dropped silver coins beside his empty jolt glass and departed without another word.

Pete Orni vigorously scrubbed several small glasses, looked at the pair of old gaffers and went back down his bar.

Three strangers came in. They were recognizable as stockmen.

They drank apart, put silver atop the bar, considered the saloon's other patrons, paid up and departed without a word.

The last visitor was old Jack Barton. He was in a hurry. He nodded around, also paid up and left. Pete Orni made a comment that was totally incorrect. 'They're gettin' ready, both factions. As for them cowmen, they'll congregate like buzzards around somethin' dead.'

As the two old men headed for the spindle doors and the roadway beyond, one of them ruefully said, 'Tomorrow'll be a good time to go up yonder to one of them lakes an' spend the day fishin'.'

Years back the saloonman had posted a sign where it would be visible from the roadway doors. It had said in large block letters that Indians were not allowed in the Blue Duck.

Similar signs existed in most saloons west of the Big River, especially in areas where reservations had been established.

Pete had removed his sign years back when Burke Arnold had taken exception to it. The Ladies Aid Society of Fleming had protested too and they might have won except for the fact that womenfolk, especially Christian ladies, never patronized saloons.

Most menfolk were indifferent. Around the Fleming countryside old Abe White Tail who had doctored the ill, two-legged and four-legged was an exception. He visited the Blue Duck when the spirit moved him, which was as often as he had been paid for performing good works.

The day before hell broke loose in Fleming he leaned on the bar and was served a mixture of popskull whiskey and ginger beer, which some townsfolk called Numb Juice, and which the local stockmen called fairy pee.

The old bronco was as solemn as Ed Bemis, the harness-making preacher, when he told Pete Orni that he'd rolled the stones and according to how they had fallen, very close to the white man's End Times was fixing to overtake Fleming and its inhabitants come sunrise tomorrow.

10

Massacre Rocks

Old Barton helped get the top buggy ready and he afterwards watched the marshal drive across to the east side alley. When he could no longer see the rig he broadly smiled. The lawman would go up the alley as far as Alice Gordon's door, which is exactly what happened. Alice came out looking as pretty as a new copper penny.

They drove northward, turned off easterly where town fencing ended and crossed open country. Rowe had a destination in mind and Alice knew where they were going. He had taken her to the same place on previous buggy rides.

There were B A cattle a fair distance northward. Too distant for the range-men watching them to be recognizable.

They were preventing the critters from drifting, something that happened when cattle had been held in one area for any length of time. When sheep grazed in one place for any length of time they cropped the feed right down to the roots. Cattle weren't that destructive, they only grazed off the tops.

Alice had brought the same hamper she had brought along other times.

Rowe made a mile wide sashay to get around the cattle and their herders. The rangemen, with little else to do, watched the rig. They didn't wave, the distance was too great but they speculated.

Rowe's destination was north-westerly several miles where there was a piddling creek and a bosque of stately ancient white oaks. It was a place favoured locally by courting couples. The stage road made a dog-leg bend in that area to avoid one of those timeless jumbles of huge boulders known among oldtimers as Massacre Rocks. Years back, a big war party of bloody-hand

Crows had ambushed a train of emigrant wagons there and had killed everyone.

The normal route would have bypassed Massacre Rocks eastward. For some reason known only to the coachmen the road had gone in the opposite direction.

The huge old rocks were visible from the creek where Rowe stopped and set down to drop the tether weight and loosen the harness.

Alice brought the hamper with her to the grassy verge and smiled at her escort as he brought over the lap robe and spread it upon a smooth area.

Directly the day would be wearing along but for now the sun was high and blessedly warm.

He shed his hat, dropped down on the blankets and helped Alice arrange the sandwiches and whatnot she had brought along.

While she was doing this in a kneeling position she did not raise her eyes to his face. Not until he mentioned the federal lawman, his prisoner, and what his predicament was.

He did not feel adamant about handing Bryan Cullom over. What he wanted was a paper releasing him from all responsibility and the federal deputy marshal not only had no such paper but did not believe one was needed.

It was the kind of a conversation a man and a woman were likely to engage in when they felt uncomfortable.

They ate and that made things easier. He brought up a subject they had discussed before and Alice said something she had joked about before.

'I'll lose a customer if we hitch horses.'

He laughed. Somewhere in the direction of those huge old rocks a horse nickered.

Rowe twisted to look over there. After a moment he said someone might have lost an animal.

Flies arrived along with a scattering of mud daubers. Getting rid of the flies wasn't difficult but mud daubers were wasps. They would sting without much provocation.

Alice carried some crusts southward. It worked, both the flies and the daubers abandoned the place where Rowe had knocked a few into the creek. The flies were not easily discouraged but they were annoying in fewer numbers.

The buggy mare pulled the light buggy with her as she grazed. When she was between the picnickers and the rocks she briefly hesitated and raised her head. For a long time she stood motionless. Rowe scooped up his hat and went closer to the creek where he could see northward without interference. He stood near some creek willows shading his eyes when Alice said, 'It's nothing.'

She could have been right. The stud-necked mare named Daisy went back to cropping grass.

Rowe rolled and lighted a smoke. Alice held up a cup. He walked back, accepted the cup and drained its contents. Lemonade was his favourite drink in hot weather.

Alice smiled upwards from her kneeling position. When he made an exaggerated gesture of pleasure she said, 'I know most of what you like and don't like.'

He handed back the empty cup, hesitated only a moment then said, 'All the more reason for us to get hitched.'

She became busy reloading the picnic hamper.

Daisy the harness mare had stopped eating again. She was standing like a statue with grass protruding from both sides of her mouth looking northward.

Alice said, 'It's something in the boulders. Prairie dog, Rowe?'

He shrugged. 'Or a coyote den.' He went back closer to the creek where visibility was better. The mare was motionless. She made no move to finish chewing the protruding grass.

Rowe approached her, patted her neck, spoke shortly to her then started back toward the place where Alice was vigorously shaking the blanket.

She folded it, took it to the buggy and put it under the seat where buggy robes were carried.

Rowe caught her hand; they walked closer to the creek and startled a small raucous bird from its nest in an oak tree.

They watched the upset small bird. Alice thought it probably had chicks because it only fled as far as another nearby oak, landed high up and scolded the two-legged intruders.

Rowe pointed to a thickly branched growth, turned Alice and kissed her. She did not resist although it had caught her by surprise. She knew about that growth high up he had pointed to. Mistletoe the time-honoured kissing plant.

She laughed a little nervously, pushed free and started back where they'd picnicked, with no reason except that she preferred not to face him until the colour in her face had subsided.

He remained in place as he called

after her. 'Alice . . . ?'

She was turning when the gunshot sounded.

It startled the big mare. She flinched but otherwise did not move. Alice saw Rowe go down. For a moment she was too stunned to react. Then she ran to him.

He tried to roll onto his side, looked up at her, said her name and collapsed.

She controlled an urge to violently shake, got an arm under him and got him into a partial sitting position. She blocked him from behind with her leg. When she pulled back the arm there was blood on her sleeve and hand. She said, 'Rowe . . . ?'

He didn't answer. She kept him in that halfway sitting position for a moment, until the shock diminished, then eased him back down, stood up and went to the big mare who stood obediently to be readied and allowed herself to be led over where Rowe was and stopped.

Alice was a strong woman, but Rowe

was a large, heavy man.

She tried to lift him. The best she could accomplish was to get him back into that sitting position.

With both hands under his arms at the shoulders she dragged him to the rig. Despite the smell of blood which ordinarily troubled horses, big Daisy did not move as Alice strained to her utmost. She got Rowe upright with bent knees, pushed as hard as she could without being able to get him into the buggy. He was a dead weight.

She had blood on her dress, hands and arms. She pleaded with Rowe to help, just a little, just enough to sag across the buggy seat.

Her strength was fading. Even without being a heavy dead weight Rowe was not positioned to raise either leg to climb up and in.

She held him with a straining heart and begged him to help. He raised his right arm, felt the buggy seat, raised his rubbery right leg and seemed ready to collapse when Alice turned sideways and threw herself in a fierce bump. Rowe fell across the seat.

Alice, with tears streaming and a set jaw, got in with no place to sit, flicked the lines and talked Daisy up into a clumsy trot in the direction of town.

When she reached the stage road she veered southward, talked the stud-necked big mare into a lope and scattered B A cattle in several directions.

Burke Arnold with two of his riders yelled and cursed. Alice neither heard nor looked around. She entered town with the top buggy swaying and jerking. People froze as she whipped past as far as the livery barn where the big mare instinctively turned in. Barton's hostler, in the act of forking feed into mangers looked up, let out a squawk and fled into the alley.

Jack came out of his harness-room-office, caught the mare, dragged her to a halt and jumped aside as he let go a bellow that could have been heard as far as Hersheimer's store.

'Jesus Christ! Alice! What happened?'

She had to be helped down. Barton got blood on himself from the effort. She breathlessly said, 'Get help. Hurry! *He's been shot!*'

Barton didn't have to go for help. People who had seen the buggy pass with the marshal's lower legs hanging out and Alice hunched over him driving the buggy like a mad person, came running.

Among the men was the US deputy marshal. He and four others got Rowe out of the rig. When they would have put him down on the barn's dirty runway, Jake Hersheimer yelled at them. 'Not on the ground! Follow me, we'll put him in the store. Is he alive?'

Alice went with the men. She glared at Hersheimer. 'Of course he's alive!'

The storekeeper used both arms to sweep away articles on his long counter, and told them to lay Rowe on it , which they did, and stood back considering the blood on their clothing. Pete Orni from the saloon said, 'What happened?'

and the federal lawman snarled at him. 'Get that shirt off him. We got to see where he got hit.'

Alice shouldered several men out of the way and went to work removing the shirt, and got more blood on her dress, hands and arms.

The marshal said, 'There it is. Storekeeper, bring some clean cloth. Lots of it.'

The lawman was surprisingly gentle. When the cloth came he sent Hersheimer for a bucket of water. More people crowded into the store. Jake Hersheimer did his best to get rid of as many as he could after putting a bucket of water on the counter where the federal marshal went to work.

Alice hovered, bloody, white as a sheet, preventing a seizure of the shakes with a strong effort.

Three riders tied up out front. The first one, Burke Arnold, brushed Jake aside. The townsmen made room for the grim-faced rangemen.

One of them leaned to examine the

marshal while simultaneously pulling off his roping gloves. He shook his head as his employer said, 'Someone fetch a bottle from the saloon.'

Burke Arnold turned from watching the marshal, faced Alice and said, 'What happened?'

It was difficult for her to keep her voice steady but she braved-up long enough to answer.

'He was in the rocks. We couldn't see him. He fired from . . . '

Arnold interrupted. 'What rocks?'

'Massacre Rocks. That's where he shot from. Rowe was at the creek.'

'How'd you get him here?'

She raised a bloody sleeve to wipe tears. 'I got him into the buggy. Don't ask me how. It just had to be done. There wasn't anyone to help.'

The cowman turned to watch the marshal being washed and said, 'Where was he hit?'

Deputy Marshal Shultz ignored the question. He spoke without taking his gaze off Burke Arnold. 'You're the feller holding that drive north of town?' Shultz paused to dry his hands. 'Mister Burke, you take your gawddamn drive out an' around this town or I'll lift your hair an' hand it out to dry.'

There wasn't a sound in the store until the B A range boss poked a rigid finger in the federal lawman's chest. He said, 'Mister Arnold drives cattle anywhere he's of a mind to.'

Shultz did not seem to move but the range boss did. He looked down where a six-gun was pushing into his middle.

The marshal made a gallows smile. 'Mister Arnold, is this here a friend of yours?'

Burke answered curtly. 'He's my range boss.'

'Well now, Mr Burke, you got a choice; take those cattle out'n around town or I gut-shoot this friend of yours for threatenin' a deputy US marshal. The law calls it self-defence.'

Arnold said, 'He didn't threaten you. Ask any of the folks standin' here.'

Shultz cocked the six-gun. 'You want

to take him back belly down or do you want to go out an' around? Mr Arnold, I've never run a bluff in my life . . . time's up!'

From back near the door partly hidden by scarcely breathing townsfolk, a clear voice carried perfectly. 'We'll go out and around, mister; what did you say your name was?'

'Woodrow Shultz, ma'am. Mind if I ask who you are?'

'Elise Arnold . . . his daughter.'

Shultz smiled. It made him almost handsome. 'Ma'am, I'm right obliged.'

Shultz leathered the weapon no one had seen him draw and pushed up to the counter where he told the range boss to cut several wide, long strips of clean cloth.

Alice left the store. People got out of her way. She paused in the opening to speak to the federal lawman.

'Will he live?'

Shultz smiled again. 'He'll live, ma'am. You folks got a doctor in Fleming?'

Elise answered looking steadily at Shultz. 'There's an old In'ian doctor. He does pretty well. I'll go find him.'

Shultz smiled again at Elise. 'I'd be real obliged, ma'am.'

Shultz told Josh Davidson to put an arm behind the marshal's shoulders and lift. While the range boss was pushing in close enough to do this, Marshal Shultz pulled down his sleeves and turned to accept the bottle of whiskey from Jake Hersheimer.

Getting whiskey down the marshal was accomplished by spilling several times the amount he swallowed. Rowe was regaining consciousness.

He raised an unsteady hand, held it out, saw the blood and put a bleary gaze upon Woodrow Shultz. The lean, grey-eyed man gently smiled and asked how Rowe felt. The answer he got came in an unsteady low voice.

'Like I been shot.'

The deputy marshal's smiled widened. 'You have been. Five, six inches more to the left an' he'd have drilled you through the heart.'

The whiskey was working. Colour appeared in Rowe's face, faint but recognizable. He looked at Josh Davidson. The range boss said, 'You got any ideal . . . ?'

Rowe's eyes made a sweep before he replied, 'How'd I get here? Jake . . . ?'

Hersheimer edged closer. 'I'm here.'

Rowe exhaled a shaky breath. 'I thought it was the store.'

Hersheimer held up the bottle. Marshal Shultz pushed it aside. He was still smiling. 'You didn't see the son of a bitch?'

'I didn't see anyone. I didn't hear anything.' Rowe took down and exhaled another breath, more steadily this time. 'Alice . . . ?'

'She went to clean up. You bled like a stuck hawg.'

'Was she hurt?'

Shultz's smile dwindled. 'No. How'n hell she got you into that buggy I'll never know. How much do you weigh?'

'Around two hunnert pounds. You

sure she's all right?'

The federal officer nodded. 'You're lucky, friend. That slug went plumb through, exited out back an' as near as I can tell from feel it didn't even crack a rib.'

Shultz nodded to the storekeeper who held up the bottle. This time there was no spillage. After the last swallow Rowe turned loose and Josh eased him back down.

Hersheimer said, 'He's got a room up at the boarding-house.'

Josh Davidson looked around, dragooned several men, all stockmen. They rolled the town marshal onto a blanket Hersheimer provided and, as the range boss growled, people stood aside and the procession carried Rowe out of the store, across the road and northward. The 'hotel's' proprietor saw them coming and scurried to open the door, peel back blankets and stand clear as Rowe was brought inside, taken to his room and placed very gently on the bed.

Josh Davidson cleared the room until only he, Burke Arnold and two or three other men remained. Jake Hersheimer put the partially emptied whiskey bottle on a nearby small table and closed the door after himself.

There was only one chair. Burke sat on it while he asked questions of which Rowe only answered a few, his unsteady voice sounding increasingly like a drowsy mumble. When he stopped speaking, closed his eyes and lay back Burke said, 'Someone go back to the store, get some bandaging cloth along with some disinfectant and fetch it back here.'

Josh Davidson moved toward the door. His employer went into the corridor with him and said, 'Not you, Josh. Someone else. You traipse out where he was shot an' see what you can find.'

The range boss departed. He passed Alice Gordon on the front porch and at her enquiring expression he said, 'Where did it happen?'

'Massacre Rocks. Is he any better?'

Josh started away as he replied, 'Go see for yourself. Alice? Did you see anythin' or hear anythin' out there?'

'Just the gunshot. It seemed to come from the rocks. Whoever he was I have no idea.'

Josh left her heading for his saddle animal and Alice went down the gloomy hallway to the half-open doorway, saw Rowe in the bed and entered.

Burke Arnold stood up and pushed the chair forward as he spoke. 'He's able to talk. The marshal here said he'll likely make it. Set down, Alice.'

She went to the edge of the bed at the exact moment Rowe opened his eyes and weakly smiled. She was wearing a fresh, clean dress. He said, 'How'd you get me into that buggy?'

She smiled. 'By straining and praying. Rowe . . . '

'I'll make it . . . You know what I was goin' to say when I got hit?'

She coloured and smiled. 'You want the answer?'

'Yes'm. Unless it'll make me hurt worse, then I don't want it.'

'Rowe? The answer is yes.'

He made a strong effort to sit up. Burke Arnold helped and got Rowe braced against the wall at his back. Rowe's colour heightened. He appeared ready to speak but she spoke first. 'I'll make supper and bring it up here.' She faced the cowman and the deputy marshal. 'I'll stay with him if you gents got other things to do.'

The lawman replied dourly, 'I'd like to join this gent's range boss an' go find the bushwhacker.'

Burke said nothing. He went with Shultz as far as the porch where Burke Arnold said, 'Mister, find the bastard an' it'll be worth a five hunnert bounty to me.'

The lean, grey-eyed man thoughtfully eyed his older companion. 'I can't take reward money, Mr Arnold, but if you wouldn't mind too much I'd like to ride out an' visit you folks.'

Arnold pushed out a work-hardened

hand. 'Any time you're in the mood, Marshal. Me'n the boys an' my daughter'd be right proud. Come at supper time. She's one hell of a cook.'

As Shultz gripped the extended hand he said, 'Is she for a fact? I'll ride out when we've found that ambushin' bastard.'

Burke Arnold watched the lean lawman walk southward in the direction of Barton's livery barn and did not see his daughter coming from the opposite direction with old Abe White Tail keeping abreast of her long-legged stride.

Where they met on the porch, Elise's father repeated what he and Marshal Shultz had spoken of.

Elise faced around and also watched the lawman. He was mid-way toward his destination. She said, 'That's right hospitable of you, Pa. I don't think there's ever before been a US marshal come visiting. Has there?'

'Never, Elise. Come along, Abe; we got a customer for you.'

The 'breed held the door for the other two. As they passed he told Burke what his daughter had told him, which was as much as she knew about the shooting.

He said no more until they were in the room where someone, probably the 'hotel's' proprietor had lighted a coal-oil lamp and had suspended it from an oversized hook in the ceiling.

Except for the Arnolds, the 'breed medicine man and the flatout marshal the room was empty.

Abe White — White Tail if only men were around — pulled the chair close, put his medicine bundle on it, went to the bedside to examine the marshal and looked around for something to sit on, found nothing and addressed Elise's father. He and Burke went back a long way. Old Abe had sat with Burke's dying wife years back and afterwards Abe had had his own ceremony at the graveside.

Someone rattled the door. Elise opened it, accepted the clean cloth and closed the door.

Abe placed the bandaging cloth at the foot of the bed and spoke without facing the cowman. 'Bad. Plenty bleeding. I put him to sleep. Bad, Burke.'

Elise's father made a short reply. 'We know it's bad, Abe. Fix it.'

'Not bad hurt, Burke, bad shot.'

11

Time's Passing

Josh Davidson and the federal marshal did not return until long after dark. The range boss turned off where the B A drive had its wagon camp. Before they split off it was possible to hear cattle. Shultz showed his humourless small smile as he addressed the range boss.

'Mister Arnold's a man as takes good advice.'

Davidson looked around. 'What does that mean, Marshal?'

'That he'll go out an' around.'

Josh snorted, reined clear and loped in the direction of B A's supper fire.

Fleming had more lights showing than it normally had even the night before it celebrated Independence Day.

Jackson Barton was asleep in his smelly combination harness room and office. Shultz cared for his animal without bothering to awaken the liveryman.

Hersheimer's store was lighted which was unusual. Jake ordinarily closed down and locked up about supper-time or maybe a bit earlier.

There was no sidewalk traffic and as Shultz emerged from the livery barn the only roadway traffic was a pair of riders who were singing an old wartime marching song, obviously having spent some time at the Blue Duck.

The marshal tried both eateries. Both were closed. He went up to the saloon and was hailed before entering from across the road where Les Welsh the stage company's corralyard boss was sufficiently visible under the harness-shop's overhang to be recognizable. There was no moon.

The federal lawman had met Welsh a few times, not well enough to be hailed by his first name.

He didn't cross over, he instead waited until the barrel-built individual crossed toward him, shook his head and said, 'We ain't acquainted but I heard about you puttin' old Arnold in his place today. If he tries to drive through town after you warned him, believe me, mister, I'll take sides with you.'

Shultz was tired and hungry. He nodded and would have brushed past but Welsh also said, 'There's talk that maybe Arnold got one of his riders to shoot the town marshal.'

'Not likely,' the federal lawman stated. 'Why would he do that?'

'You don't know that old bastard. Drivin' through town is a sort of ritual with him, an' he's not a feller who cottons to bein' warned off.'

Shultz took his time appraising the other man. 'You got an interest, friend?' he asked.

'Just that it's time he had some slack yanked out of him.'

Shultz pushed past. 'We'll see come morning,' he stated and entered the Blue Duck where three large lamps made the saloon twice as light as day.

At the bar, a pair of townsmen made room and nodded. Pete Orni set up a bottle and a glass, leaned and said, 'Find anything?'

Shultz was pouring when he shook his head. 'Some tracks is all.'

Pete waited until the first drink had been splashed on its way down before speaking again. 'The marshal's worse'n when you last seen him.'

Shultz put down the glass and pushed the bottle away. 'He didn't look real good. Did the old man's girl fetch an' In'ian to tend him?'

'Abe White Tail? He's been doctorin' around the countryside since I come here. What Rowe needs is a real doctor.'

'Where's the nearest one?'

'Up at Clausberg, fifty, sixty miles north. He'll be dead before anyone can make it up there an' back.'

The deputy marshal went up to the rooming-house and met Alice in the hallway. She nodded and would have passed but he stopped her with the question she'd been asked at least a dozen times.

'How is he?'

'Abe's got him sleeping. I did the bandaging. I don't know how Abe does that but it works. I was a midwife's helper for him some years ago. The woman slept through without so much as a groan.'

'You reckon it'd be all right if I looked in on him?'

Alice turned to accompany Shultz to the room she had just left.

Someone, probably the rooming-house owner had turned the lamp down low. When she and Shultz entered, Rowe was sitting up in the bed, eyes open. He smiled at them. He was bandaged from the top of his chest downward. It looked like a professional job.

The marshal went to the bedside to return Rowe's greeting where he said, 'The B A range boss an' me went up yonder an' prowled all around those rocks where it seems someone tried to kill you.'

Rowe's voice was firm when he said, 'Find anything?'

'Nothing,' Shultz replied. 'Old sign, cattle, bare-foot horses, most likely wild ones. No boot prints an' no spent casing. It don't prove that's not where he was.'

Alice quietly said, 'That's where I saw smoke, and the buggy mare kept looking over there.'

Shultz shrugged. 'I'm goin' back there in the morning. Right now I could sleep a week standin' up.'

Rowe was diffident. 'You got no cause to waste your time lookin' for him, Woody.'

Shultz showed that small smile again. 'I got to see you on your feet. I can't take Cullom north unless you release him to me.'

From the doorway Shultz drily said, 'When you're up an' around maybe between the two of us . . . Rowe, you know the country and the folks.'

After the door closed behind the

grey-eyed lawman, Alice said, 'Isn't there some way you can give him your prisoner, Rowe?'

'Not without him showing the legal papers signed by the governor. I can't just up and hand Cullom over.'

She arose, smoothed her skirt, kissed him on the cheek, promised to bring breakfast in the morning and departed.

Rowe cocked his head until he heard the roadway door open and close then dug out the whiskey bottle from beneath his blankets and tipped it. It was painful when he moved, especially where old Abe White had pulled torn flesh to be cinched together.

The following day he had more women visitors than men. They volunteered to do his laundry, give him a bath, which he swore he could do by himself, if they would haul the water and bring him a cake of soap.

The old 'breed arrived short of noon. In some ways Abe White Tail clung to Indian ways. In other ways he copied the whiteskins he lived among. He kept his hair cut short and except for ankle-high moccasins his outer attire came from Hersheimer's clothing section.

No one, including Abe, knew how old he was. For an Indian, full blood or 'breed, to be respected by whiteskins he had to earn it and Abe had done that years ago with his cures and his ability to set bones and correctly diagnose ailments. For every woman with a hung-up baby that old Abe had delivered there were no more than a handful who hadn't needed the old bronco.

Abe was a slightly stooped, quiet individual. He neither carried tales nor repeated confidences.

One time Pete Orni told Les Welsh the old 'breed probably knew enough about folks in the Fleming countryside to fill a croaker sack.

When Abe appeared at the rooming-house shortly after Alice had departed with the tray and dishes from Rowe's breakfast, the town marshal watched as

Abe pulled up the room's solitary chair, sat down, considered the wounded man with the solemnity of an owl and said, 'You make it fine. Plenty good women take care of you. Other man don't do so good. Sometimes out of head.'

Rowe nodded. He not only had no idea what Abe was talking about he didn't care. With a full stomach after not having slept well the night before he could have agreed to just about anything in order to outwait a visitor and sleep.

The old man squirmed on the chair to get more comfortable and gazed at the marshal with a pair of jet-black eyes which in their impassive manner suggested he was in no hurry to depart, not even when Rowe very carefully eased up onto one side with his back to Abe White Tail.

Eventually the 'breed arose and went to stand by the room's only window. He remained over there for a long time watching roadway traffic, women with knit shopping bags entering Hersheimer's store and spoke again without facing around.

'They don't find him. They don't read sign, otherwise they track to my house. He got plenty blood from his head. I put him to bed in blankets. He talk. Make no sense but keep talkin'. I put him together. Had to make him sleep first. Bad hurt.'

Abe turned to face into the room. His friend the marshal was snoring.

Abe left. The man who kept horses at the lower end of town had a sick horse.

Anyone who had spent most of a long life with animals should know croup from founder but Jack Barton didn't, so when Abe arrived at the barn, examined the horse and told Barton his ailing animal should be shod and re-shod every thirty days with spreader shoes in front, Barton nodded with the assurance of someone who wouldn't admit ignorance. He gave Abe a two-bit piece and told him he had known it wasn't croup all the time.

Abe pocketed the money, smiled and departed.

Up at the Blue Duck, he told Pete Orni that white men didn't know the difference between being a horseman and someone who simply used animals, to which Pete agreed without having any idea what the old 'breed was talking about.

Abe was leaving the saloon with a small warmth in his stomach and saw Alice carrying a wicker hamper on her way to the rooming-house. She waved and Abe waved back, shook his head and went shuffling toward the abandoned slab shack where he lived.

The rooming-house proprietor met Alice, held the door for her to enter the marshal's room and continued to hold it open when the US deputy marshal came along in Alice's footsteps. After the lawman was also inside, the rooming-house man closed the door, wagged his head and went to his living-quarters in the southernmost part of his old building which had once, years earlier, been an army barracks.

Rowe was sitting up. Alice acknowledged the federal marshal's presence with a cheerful smile, put her hamper on the only chair, rummaged until she found what she sought, then, with her back to the marshal, went to work mixing soap and water to make a frothy mix and told Rowe to sit still as she lathered his face and briefly hesitated holding the ivory-handled straight razor poised.

Deputy Marshal Shultz watched in silence as Rowe was shaved. He waited until Alice was finished then told her she had done as good a job as a real-life barber would have done.

Shultz talked while Alice fed Rowe from her wicker hamper. His first scrap of information was welcome; it settled one of the town's problems. 'Old Arnold's got his drive gathered and he's going westerly out and around your town.'

Alice had seen and heard the gather

being bunched with the leaders following B A's range boss going west. She hadn't lingered to watch the range boss change course out a ways to lead the drive southward.

Marshal Shultz had watched from his position out front of the saloon, leaning on an overhang upright. He waited until Josh Davidson made his southward sashay from about a half-mile out before heading for the rooming-house.

Rowe ate like a bitch wolf, acknowledged what his visitors had to say with up and down shakes of his head and did not speak until he was finished eating.

While Alice was reloading her hamper, Marshal Shultz said he was going to return to Massacre Rocks in the hope that with broad daylight rather than the diminishing light he and Josh Davidson had been required to use the previous day he might be able to find some sign.

After Shultz left, Alice sat on the edge of Rowe's bed to change the bandaging. Rowe did not object although he didn't believe the bandaging needed changing.

Alice carefully removed the wrapping, examined the wounds and without probing them where swelling and faint discoloration was noticeable, used water from the bucket that had been brought the previous day to wash Rowe, who tried without success to stifle a gasp. The water was as cold as a witch's bosom.

She laughed at him. When he was dried and rebandaged she arose, kissed him and departed. Rowe had not noticed the expression of anxiety nor were the wounds any more painful than they had been before despite a slight sensation of fever at the swellings.

Alice went looking for Abe White Tail. One of the hostlers at the corralyard told her he had seen the old 'breed heading toward the lower end of town where he had his shack.

She returned to the café where hungry men arrived singly and in pairs, personally and privately worried over what she had seen while rebandaging the marshal.

Marshal Shultz returned after dark. His second search for signs where the bushwhacker had fired from hiding were cursory. He had ridden to the sprawling yard of Burke Arnold's ranch where he and Burke's daughter had visited.

She had shown him her personal string of horses which Shultz had no difficulty admiring, not entirely because they were handsome animals but also because he was fond of horses.

When he left, Elise's father loped into the yard with a redheaded companion. Elise told her father who the visitor had been and he asked if the federal marshal had come to ask questions. She smiled as she told him it had been a purely social visit.

All the way back to town Marshal Shultz told his horse it was time both of them worked out some arrangement where neither of them would have to travel all over hell doing lawman's work.

When he went to look in on Rowe he truthfully said that whoever the bushwhacker was, he was seasoned at hiding tracks.

Over at the café, Alice's last customer had departed and she was cleaning up when the US marshal walked in, sat at the counter and asked if it was too late to be fed.

She went to the kitchen, returned with two platters, set them in front of her latest customer and answered as best she could the questions he asked, which had very little to do with the town marshal or his ambusher.

Later, when she was alone she locked the roadway door, doused the light and went to her lean-to, beginning to reconsider her earlier opinion of the government lawman.

The following day, she saw Marshal Shultz leave town by the northerly stage road, went over to the rooming-house with breakfast for Rowe and was stopped by the preacher-harness-maker who told her, as he had told others, how pleased he was that the B A cattle had not gone through town. He also told her Abe the 'breed medicine man had been looking for her.

She had been looking for him and hadn't found him. It would have to wait.

Rowe greeted her with a wide smile. Her smile was slightly restrained. He wasn't sure the bandaging needed changing but she was insistent, and when she had peeled it all away she sat on the edge of the bed regarding both wounds with an unreadable expression.

She was less talkative than usual while the rebandaging was being done.

He asked what was troubling her and she smiled as she answered.

'Your recovery.'

He sloughed that off. 'I heal fast. Always have, even when I was a kid.' He cocked his head a little. 'Ma'am, I'd sure admire to take you buggy ridin' when I'm able.'

She smiled without enthusiasm, stood up and kissed him, twice, left the hotel and was entering the café when she saw the old 'breed slowly walking north from the lower end of town. She waited. When he shuffled more slowly and would have passed she said, 'Abe, come inside with me. I'll fix you some breakfast.'

The old man brightened. As he perched at the counter she called from the kitchen.

'Have you been to see the marshal?'

He called back. 'I was on my way. From here I'll go up there.'

As she set the laden platter in front of him she continued to lean as she spoke. 'It's getting red around the wounds. Red an' swollen.'

He chewed a long time before looking up and speaking. 'That why I go today. It's time.'

She remained bent, both hands palms down atop the counter.

'Infection?'

He wiped his lips and stood up. 'No

worry until day after tomorrow. Then we both worry.'

She caught him at the door. 'I'll send for the doctor at Clausberg.'

Old Abe smiled indulgently. 'You worry. Wait. Wait for tomorrow.'

When the old bronco entered his room Rowe held up a hand. 'I already been rewrapped. Washed an' rewrapped.'

Abe White Tail grinned his way to the edge of the bed where he gingerly sat and reached with both hands to untie the bandaging.

Rowe protested. The old man's grin was fixed. He worked at removing everything Alice had only recently put on. When Rowe was sufficiently bare Abe leaned to gently probe. Because his eyesight was no longer as it once had been he had to lean close.

To Rowe it seemed not only an unnecessary examination but a pro-longed one. But he did not complain not even when the old man pinched and scraped the wounds, sat back grinning like a tame ape and removed the parfleche from his belt, palmed what appeared to be tiny leaves and dirt, rolled whatever it produced, leaned and sprinkled the evil smelling dust on both injuries, massaged them gently and began rewrapping the bandaging.

He only stopped grinning as he wiped both palms on the outside of his trousers and stood up. Now, finally, his features resumed their normal expression.

Rowe fidgeted. 'What the hell was that? Smells worse'n a tanyard.'

Abe ignored the question. 'It don't hurt?'

'It sort of feels hot. What was it?'

Abe resecured the parfleche to his belt, hesitated then went to the door. He turned, smiled and said, 'Tomorrow I come back.'

An hour later, Alice and Marshal Shultz arrived. Rowe greeted the lawman as a friend but otherwise ignored him to tell Alice about the old 'breed's visit. She nodded and smiled but said nothing because, although she had known of Abe White Tail's other cures, while she believed he was capable enough with sprains, cuts, bruises and birthing babies, what she wanted to believe and what common sense told her to be sceptical of, she neither asked questions nor forgot to be encouraging when she spoke. All she said was something to the effect that all her life she had heard about Indian medicine being half fantasy and half fact.

Marshal Shultz put in his two bits' worth while looking steadily at the younger man in the bed.

'Up in Montana I've seen them medicine men set bones an' patch holes as good as any whiteskin could've done. After all, Rowe, you want to remember them tomahawks been around longer'n we have an' given that much time they've figured things we don't know about.'

Alice promised to bring dinner later and departed. Her intention was to seek old Abe for an explanation but she didn't go to his shack south of the livery barn upon the opposite side of the road a few yards below the smithy.

Marshal Shultz lingered with Rowe. Without saying it he left the town marshal with the impression that the bushwhacker was not going to be found; by now he'd had time enough if he rode hard to be so distant in any one of four directions they might as well forget him and concentrate on Rowe's recovery.

Rowe grudgingly conceded. For a fact, every day he remained bed-ridden the ambusher would be increasing the distance between them.

12

Death and Life

Burke Arnold told his range boss he thought his daughter's pride and joy, the stocking-legged chestnut horse was acting like he had a case of the cramps.

Davidson went to examine the horse and told his employer the chestnut acted like it had a wired gut. Where Davidson had put pressure the horse had flinched. Josh recommended a grain mixture mixed with the kind of sour medicine that induced heaving.

Burke told the range boss to go to town and bring back Abe White Tail. He also told Davidson not to mention any of this to his daughter.

When Josh Davidson arrived in Fleming he tied up out front of the Blue Duck; if the old 'breed wasn't there Pete Orni might know where he was.

The saloonman said he'd been in long enough to down a jolt and had left in the direction of the rooming-house.

It had been the range boss's intention, as long as he had to come to town anyway, to pay the town marshal a visit.

When he got over there he found the federal marshal helping Alice reload a wicker hamper. She had brought breakfast to Rowe and had to hasten back to the café where her regulars would be congregating.

Josh had to stand, the lawman had the chair. He told Rowe he looked a hundred per-cent better than he had looked the last time they'd met.

Rowe also felt better. He told the two men what the old 'breed had done with the awful-smelling concoction from his parfleche.

Josh cut his visit short. He had to locate the old man and it was a long ride back. He had another reason, but neither Shultz nor the town marshal knew it. Josh had cheeked a cud before leaving the ranch. It was chewed out. He got as far as the front porch before jettisoning the tobacco in the direction of a sickly looking geranium plant before continuing his search for Abe White Tail.

Marshal Shultz also left the rooming-house, not to pursue his manhunt for a bushwhacker, but to make another long ride. He had prepared for it before breakfast. His boots were freshly dusted and rubbed, his coat and britches had been brushed until the dust no longer flew.

He was walking southward in the direction of the livery barn when he met the range boss. They walked together.

Josh told the lawman he'd been informed at Hersheimer's store Abe had been in shortly before to buy medicine, some components for one of his own concoctions and a large roll of bandaging cloth.

The marshal's comment was logically

given. 'He's got to be doctorin'. From what I've heard he's downright good at healin' folks.'

Josh had not only heard the same thing, he had seen evidence of it.

He told the marshal of cures he'd seen, the old man's accomplishments and when they were in front of the livery barn's wide opening the marshal's curiosity made him say, 'If he's that good I'll go with you. I got a saddle sore that bothers me now'n then.'

Old Abe opened the door for them and both men momentarily recoiled from the odour.

Abe stepped aside for them to enter. Abe's shack had two doors, one in front, one in back, but no windows. During decent weather Abe kept the rear door open for light. It was when Abe's visitors entered and closed the front door after them that dimness returned.

There were several tins for candles. One was lighted in a small room, evidently an afterthought by the shack's original builder whoever he might have been.

The poor visibility took second place to the smell; both Abe's visitors did not move very far from the door. Abe had been feeding kindling into his makeshift stove when his visitors had arrived.

He went back to feeding the stove. On one side of the stove someone's discarded chair was draped with drying clothing.

Josh Davidson's gaze was fixed on the chair. When the marshal mentioned his occasional saddle sore trouble, Josh moved toward the stove.

While the other two men talked, Josh gingerly removed a drying garment from the chair, held it to the light as he examined it, put it back on the chair and said, 'Abe, is this your shirt?'

The 'breed looked from the shirt to the range boss and shook his head. 'Belong him,' he said. Jutting his jaw in the direction of the candlelit adjoining room.

The range boss went over to the door

and stopped in the opening. He turned slowly. 'Abe? Who is he? What happened to him?'

The 'breed's answer was given candidly. 'Found him crawling in the alley. He been hurt bad. Brought him here.'

'Who is he, Abe?'

'Never said name.' Abe edged in the doorway, looked in and spoke again. 'He bad hurt. I make him sleep.'

The range boss returned to the chair, re-examined the shirt and when the old man said, 'I wash shirt three times. Too much blood,' the range boss returned to the doorway, stepped inside, picked up a saddle gun, levered it, leaned it aside and stood over the man on the pile of old robes and pursed his lips.

Marshal Shultz said, 'You know him?'

Davidson answered without looking away from the sleeping man on the earthen floor. 'I know that shirt. The last time I saw anyone wearin' it was up yonder where someone had Elise Arnold an' Alice Gordon prisoner. We left him for dead.' Davidson turned. 'Abe, where's he hurt?'

The 'breed pushed past, leaned and touched the thick, unprofessional bandage. 'Head,' he said. 'Head . . . bad hurt. You know him?'

Josh Davidson didn't reply; he went back to the chair and held up the bloodstained shirt. 'How the hell,' he said, 'did the son of a bitch get down here? Marshal, I'll give you big odds . . . ' Davidson dropped the shirt back onto a chair. 'I got no idea how he did it. We left him for dead up yonder. I'll give you odds he got into those rocks an' shot Rowe.'

Shultz went to examine the bandaged man. He raised up slowly. 'Are you sayin' he crawled all that way carryin' that Winchester an' got hid in them rocks?'

'That's what I'm sayin'.' Davidson faced the 'breed. 'You back-tracked him, Abe?'

White Tail nodded. 'Up to where he got onto the road. From there to out back of my house. He . . . comes to an' talks, then faints. I doctored him for last three days.' Abe stood over the sleeping man, who was filthy and stained with dried blood. 'He don't stay awake long. Feel his head.'

Neither the lawman nor the range boss offered to comply. Davidson left by the alley doorway, quartered until he found the sign and tracked it northerly before turning back. Inside, he ignored Shultz to ask Abe questions which the old man answered candidly, but he had no idea how the man he had found in sprawled unconsciousness in the alley behind his house had got there.

Davidson forgot his reason for coming to town. He dropped the stained shirt, sat on a chair and looked past the other two people into the feebly lighted room where Abe's latest 'patient' was lying.

Eventually he stood up. 'I got to tell the town marshal, he said. 'Abe, don't let him out of your sight.'

After both his visitors had departed,

Abe went to finish his chore of feeding the stove, picked up the stained shirt and shook his head. He didn't have to be told to watch his guest; Abe White Tail had doctored too many injured people in his lifetime not to know when one was not going to stand up from his pallet of hair-on fur hides.

Marshal Shultz left the range boss, got his horse and left town riding northward. If the shot had come from Massacre Rocks and he had searched every yard of that area then either B A's range boss was wrong or the shirt hadn't been worn by the 'breed's guest.

Davidson returned to the rooming-house to tell the town marshal what he had found and had to awaken Rowe to do it.

Rowe listened patiently. 'Tracks, Josh. You'n the marshal didn't find any. Maybe what Abe found in the alley wasn't the real bushwhacker.'

Josh Davidson hadn't yielded a conviction since childhood. He didn't yield now. 'Rowe, I got no idea how he did it. That's one hell of a distance from that log house to town . . . to them rocks . . . but no one else was wearin' that shirt. He wanted you dead the worst way. I've known men driven damned near to death to keep a promise.'

Their discussion did not evolve into an argument. Rowe was willing to believe, he just could not for the life of him figure how that half-dead man they'd left up yonder had got all the way down to Massacre Rocks, which had to be a distance of close to six miles, in the shape he'd been in when Rowe had last seen him. He asked the range boss if there had been horse tracks from up yonder to the rocks. Davidson hadn't gone back to the clearing looking for sign. He privately promised himself he would do that. He said, 'I told you, Rowe, that was the shirt he was wearing. If there was another one like it that wouldn't account for the blood.' Davidson arose when Alice arrived with her hamper.

He returned to the 'breed's shack, told Abe about Elise's horse and the old man said he would go up there immediately if Josh would mind his sick man in the back room while Abe was gone.

Davidson agreed. After Abe had left, he went to squat beside the pallet where the man with the bandaged head was sleeping.

He whittled off a sliver from his plug, cheeked it and spat aside.

The candle didn't help, nor was it needed. The sun was high, shafts of it got through a dozen cracks.

Abe used whiskey in some of his medicinal concoctions. The bottle was atop a small wooden crate where the candle also stood.

Josh got a swallow for himself and hesitated about replacing the bottle.

The filthy, ragged and unwashed man on the pallet groaned in his sleep.

Davidson asked him his name. There was no reply, just another groan, slightly stronger this time.

Josh pulled the pallet until one of those shafts of sunlight was on the other man's face.

The next time there was a groan it was followed by words.

'Dead . . . centre . . . through the . . . lights.'

Josh leaned, held the bottle poised and said, 'Swallow. You hear me?'

The man's eyes barely flickered as he opened and closed his mouth. The range boss leaned more, pulled the stopper with his teeth and said it again. 'Swallow!'

The eyes closed, but the mouth moved as it had before and Davidson trickled from the bottle. Conscious or unconscious a person instinctively swallowed when his mouth was full.

The man on the pallet swallowed once, coughed and swallowed twice more. He rolled his head sideways and Josh leaned back with the bottle.

Davidson tried once more. 'What is your name?'

Miracle of miracles he got an answer.

'Chris Humes. Where is she?'

'Where is who?'

The bandaged man's breathing was shallowly uneven. He partially closed his eyes.

Davidson stood up, replaced the bottle on the wooden crate beside the glowing candle and went into the other room. Either he was becoming accustomed to that foul odour or it was dissipating. He sat on the chair, held the stained shirt to another penetrating shaft of sunlight, carefully examined the shirt, found a scrap of paper in a shirt pocket, worked it free from the cloth, unfolded it very carefully and although at one time there had been some scribbling on it and while it had survived being soaked through with blood and later with wash water, whatever had been written on it had not. He held it to the light, smoothed gently, held it close, even tried holding it above the stove. Nothing he did helped, the scribbling was hopelessly unreadable.

He got rid of his cud in the stove and as he straightened around from doing this, a shadow filled the front doorway. It spoke before Davidson could. 'Where is he? Rowe told me.'

Davidson jerked his head in the direction of the small room and watched her stop in the doorway and remain motionless until he said, 'Sleepin'. I gave him some whiskey. I think Abe got some of his medicine down him before that. He comes around an' passes out.'

Alice entered the little room, stood a moment looking down before she knelt.

The range boss remained in the other room by the fire until she appeared in the doorway round eyed and pale.

'Josh?'

'Yes'm.'

'He's dead . . . '

The range boss covered the intervening distance in long strides, knelt for a long moment before arising to face her. 'He . . . tried to talk minutes ago.'

She went to the chair, sat and slowly

leaned to pick up the shirt. She held it up and spoke from behind it. 'He's the one that kept us prisoners up yonder. Elise Arnold caught him from behind with an iron skillet.'

Alice let the shirt fall. 'How did he get here?'

Davidson answered candidly. 'I got no idea. My guess is that he somehow got down here. He had a carbine. He . . . I think it was him maybe restin' in them rocks, saw you'n the marshal an' shot him. Abe found him out back in the alley some days back. He's been doctorin' him.'

Alice arose and departed without a word. She walked all the way to the rooming-house, entered the marshal's room without knocking and began talking.

Rowe stopped her with an upraised hand. 'If it was him in the rocks, how did he get there from up yonder where he was left bleedin' like a dyin' bull?'

She neither had an answer nor any idea, but she believed he had been in the rocks, believed it to her dying day.

So did Josh Davidson. The federal marshal said he wanted to believe it, but he'd known tough men in his time, tough, unrelenting, unyielding and not a one of them could have held together to ride or walk or crawl from the log house to the outskirts of Fleming in the condition that tinhorn rustler had been after he got hit over the head with an iron fry pan.

Rowe was recovering to everyone's satisfaction, but he was unable to be up and about so he asked Alice to visit Bryan Cullom at the jailhouse, tell him Chris Humes was dead and return to tell Rowe what Cullom's reaction had been.

She did it but not until it was dinnertime and she had a legitimate reason to go to the jailhouse; she had been feeding him since the town marshal's bushwhack.

After she'd taken food to Cullom they had talked while he ate. Whether because the prisoner felt beholden or because he welcomed an opportunity to unload, he told her everything he knew about both his dead partners in the rustling enterprise and as much more as he knew about them personally.

Rowe was satisfied. As had happened with his prisoner, as he ate he listened and when she finished talking and he finished eating while she was putting things back in the hamper with her back to him, he asked her a question and made a statement. 'I been practisin' walkin' an' exercisin' some. Alice?'

She turned holding the basket. He spoke in a firm voice. He had been practising this too.

'Will you marry me?'

She placed the hamper on the chair, went to the bedside, kissed him squarely on the mouth and pulled back. 'You need another shave. I'll bring the soap and razor in the morning.'

He stared without moving or making a sound. She went as far as the door before turning back. 'Yes. When?'

'Tell the preacher to come with you in the mornin'.'

She nodded, threw him a kiss and closed the door after herself. Rowe pushed back the blankets, stood up, went to the window and watched her enter the café. He blew out a ragged breath and was starting in the direction of the bed when the federal deputy marshal walked in. He didn't knock either.

He stood stone still for a moment before speaking. 'You better get back in that bed.'

Rowe went that far but sat on the edge of the bed, did not get into it. He said, 'You met her on the way out?'

Shultz nodded.

'We got a preacher in Fleming.'

Shultz nodded about that. 'I met him durin' that tussle over the cattle drive.'

'He's goin' to marry us in the morning.'

Shultz gazed at the town marshal a long time before speaking. 'That's what you been doin', practisin' standin' up?'

Before Rowe could answer the lawman spoke again. 'That feller that shot you . . . he died down at the old bronco's cabin.'

Rowe nodded. 'I know.'

'Well, I got a paper from up north authorizin' you to hand Cullom over to me to be taken up north an' tried in a court.'

Shultz handed Rowe a folded letter-type missive. Rowe put it behind him on the bed, something Shultz watched him do without comment. He had something more to say. 'You keep him locked up until another deputy marshal gets here.' At Rowe's blank look, Shultz smiled and stood up. 'I sent 'em my resignation.' Rowe's expression did not change. 'Elise Arnold'n I been ridin' out now'n then. She wants me to stay.'

Rowe digested this and its implications slowly. From what he knew of the disposition of old Burke's daughter . . . he smiled, arose from the edge of the bed and held out his hand.

They gripped hands, pumped once

and released the grip. Marshal Shultz sat back down in the chair before speaking again. 'What I really came here to tell you — about that dead one named Humes — some grub-line rider named Hampton heard the ruckus up at the log cabin, hid in the forest until everyone rode past then snuck back there to rummage whatever wasn't tied down. Your bushwhacker caught him, took his horse and rode after you. How'd I know this? Me'n Elise went ridin' an' found him on foot. I took him up behind me an' headed back. It was dark when we got to her yard. She gave him a horse an' he rode off. Rowe, I haven't eaten since Hector was a pup.'

Shultz stood up wearing a little crooked smile. 'I got to congratulate your friend. She's a right good cook.'

After the marshal departed, Rowe returned to the window and watched Shultz heading for the eatery.

We do hope that you have enjoyed reading this large print book.

Did you know that all of our titles are available for purchase?

We publish a wide range of high quality large print books including:
Romances, Mysteries, Classics
General Fiction
Non Fiction and Westerns

Special interest titles available in large print are:
The Little Oxford Dictionary
Music Book, Song Book
Hymn Book, Service Book

Also available from us courtesy of Oxford University Press:
Young Readers' Dictionary
(large print edition)
Young Readers' Thesaurus
(large print edition)

For further information or a free brochure, please contact us at:
Ulverscroft Large Print Books Ltd.,
The Green, Bradgate Road, Anstey,
Leicester, LE7 7FU, England.
Tel: (00 44) **0116 236 4325**
Fax: (00 44) **0116 234 0205**

Other titles in the
Linford Western Library:

STONE MOUNTAIN

Concho Bradley

The stage robbery had been accomplished by an old woman. Twine Fourch had never heard of a female being a highway robber before. He followed the trail all the way to a dilapidated log cabin up Stone Mountain. What happened after that no one could believe even after townsmen from Jefferson found the old log house and the skeletal dying old woman. But before the mystery could be solved there would be two unnecessary killings, a bizarre suicide and a lynching.

GUNS OF THE GAMBLER

M. Duggan

Destitute gambler Ben Crow arrives in Mallory keen to claim his inheritance, only to discover that rancher Edward Bacon has other ideas. Set up by Miss Dorothy, who had fooled him completely, Ben finds himself dangling on the end of a rope. Saved from death, Ben sets off in pursuit of Miss Dorothy, determined upon retribution. However, his quest for vengeance turns into a rescue mission when she is kidnapped by a crazy man-burning bandit.

SIDEWINDER

John Dyson

All Flynn wants is to be Marshal of Tucson, but he is framed by the territory's richest rancher, Frank Buchanan, and thrown into Yuma prison. Five years later Flynn comes out, intent on clearing his name and burning for vengeance. Fists thud, knives flash and bullets fly as he rides both sides of the law and participates in kidnapping and double-dealing. He is once again arrested for a murder of which he is innocent. Can he escape the noose a second time?

THE BLOODING OF JETHRO

Frank Fields

When Jethro Smith's family is murdered by outlaws, vengeance is the one thing on his mind. He meets the brother of one of the murderers, who attempts to exploit Jethro's grudge in the pursuit of his own vendetta. The local preacher, formerly a sheriff, teaches Jethro how to use a gun. With his new-found skills, Jethro and his somewhat unwelcome friend pit themselves against seemingly impossible odds. Whatever the outcome lead would surely fly.

SEVEN HELLS AND A SIXGUN

Jack Greer

Jim Cayman had been warned about Daphne Rankin, his boss's wife, and her little ways. When Daphne made a play for Jim and he resisted, the result was painful and about what he had feared. But suddenly matters went beyond the expected and he found himself left to die an awful death. Only then did he realise that there was far more than a woman scorned. He vowed that if he could escape from the hell-hole he would surely solve the mystery — and settle some scores.